TAKING AIM

POWER AND PAIN, TEENS AND GUNS

EDITED BY
MICHAEL CART

WITHDRAWN

STAKING AIM

POWER AND PAIN,
TEENS AND GUNS

HARPER TEEN
An Imprint of HarperCollinsPublishers

HarperTeen is an imprint of HarperCollins Publishers.

Taking Aim: Power and Pain, Teens and Guns
Compilation copyright © 2015 by Michael Cart
Introduction copyright © 2015 by Michael Cart
"A Culture of Guns . . . with Comments from Sons" © 2015 by Marc Aronson, Will Weaver, and Chris Crutcher
"Roach" © 2015 by the Estate of Walter M. Myers
"Embraced by Raven Arms" © 2015 by Tim Wynne-Jones
"Shoot" © 2015 by Gregory Galloway
"The Bodyguard: A Fable" © 2015 by Ron Koertge
"Fight or Flight" © 2015 by Alex Flinn
"Certified Deactivated" © 2015 by Chris Lynch
"Love Packs Heat" © 2015 by Eric Shanower
"The Dragon" © 2015 by Francesca Lia Block
"The Babysitters" © 2015 by Jenny Hubbard
"The Battle of Elphinloan" © 2015 by Elizabeth Gatland
"Dark Hobby" © 2015 by Edward Averett
"The Gunslinger" © 2015 by Peter Johnson
"Heartbreak" by Joyce Carol Oates © 2015 by The Ontario Review, Inc.

Library of Congress Cataloging-in-Publication Data
    Taking aim : power and pain, teens and guns / edited by Michael Cart.
        pages   cm
    Summary: "This anthology of stories from acclaimed young adult authors examines the thought-provoking issues of gun violence, gun control, and gun ownership"— Provided by publisher.
    ISBN 978-0-06-232735-2 (hardback)
    1. Firearms—Juvenile fiction. 2. Short stories, American. [1. Firearms—Fiction. 2. Short stories.]   I. Cart, Michael, editor.
PZ5.T179 2015   2015005621
[Fic]—dc23   CIP
                                                AC

Typography by Ellice M. Lee
15 16 17 18 19   CG/RRDH   10 9 8 7 6 5 4 3 2 1
❖
First Edition

For Marcia, sister and friend

CON

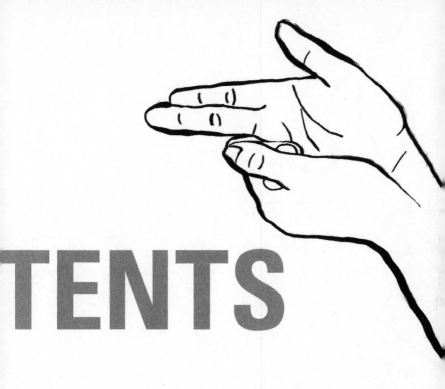

TENTS

INTRODUCTION

There is a picture of me taken when I was seven or eight. In it I'm dressed in full cowboy regalia from head to toe, from cowboy hat, that is, to cowboy boots. Wrapped around my middle is a belt holding twin holsters, and in each holster is a shiny new cap gun. Understand that I was no anomaly; there must be countless pictures of other kids dressed and armed just like me, for it was an era of popular cowboy movies boasting such stalwart heroes as Roy Rogers (my favorite), Gene Autry, Hopalong Cassidy, and more. These gun-toting, white-hat-wearing good guys were emblems of an American gun culture rooted in the American frontier, though I didn't know it at the time. I only remember playing cowboys; the object of the game being to shoot your friends ("Gotcha!" "No, you didn't!" "Yes, I did!" "No, I ducked!"). Happily, we all survived the pretend mayhem. Several years passed and I was newly armed, this time with a BB gun, and my quarry was no longer my friends but, instead, big game—lions, and tigers, and bears, oh my. In my imagination I had become a mighty hunter, another manifestation of gun culture. In truth, my father took me hunting only once and that was for small game: rabbits, as I recall. I was armed with my BB gun, and he with the shotgun that was kept in the unlocked closet in the family room along with a deer rifle. We returned home empty-handed that day. I had better luck—if that's the word—several years after that when I borrowed a friend's pellet gun and shot (and killed) a bird. I was so dismayed and guilt-ridden by the act that I gave up guns of any sort until, as a young adult, I became a soldier and was forced to learn how to operate the real thing, an M14 rifle. Mercifully I never had to use it in combat, since I was assigned unarmed duty as a librarian and military historian! But I remember holding the wretched thing on the rifle range ("Ready on the right? Ready on the left? Ready on the firing line.") and shuddering, for, frankly, I was afraid of the thing and of the violence it could wreak. If guns had not been anathema to me before, they certainly were after my army experience.

When my father died, my mother—instead of getting rid of the blamed things—gave the guns to my nephew, who is a hunter. Also hunters are my niece's husband and their two sons. As a result, my feelings about guns have become a bit more ambivalent. On the one hand, I'd be quite happy to see all firearms outlawed; but on the other hand, I know there are countless other Americans who, like my nephews and great-nephews, use them responsibly for sport. Should those be banned? If not, how can they be kept out of the hands of irresponsible or unwell people? This is a serious matter, one might say a matter of life and death, since, according to the *New York Times*, an estimated one-third of American children live in homes with firearms and 43 percent have at least one unlocked firearm available. Surely related to this is the sad fact that since the Columbine tragedy in 1999, some of the most significant cases of shootings—Virginia Tech, Tucson, Aurora, Newtown—have all been perpetrated by young adults.

These are questions and issues that are firing an ongoing and heated debate about the place of guns in American society. To shed light as well as heat on this issue, I've invited sixteen leading authors for young adults to create stories about guns and gun culture. They responded, as I hoped, with art and insight, examining virtually every aspect of the topic.

In the book's opening, Marc Aronson, Will Weaver, and Chris Crutcher set the stage for the stories that follow by writing brief essays about guns in the context of their families and America's gun culture. Following them is a dark story by the late Walter Dean Myers about a boy whose abysmally low self-esteem is impacted when a gun comes into his possession and the potential for violence ensues in a culture beyond caring.

Pair this with the ironic story by Tim Wynne-Jones, where a gun comes almost magically into the hands of a boy who has been brutally bullied and as a result, however briefly, the perpetrator becomes the victim.

Hunting is an integral part of gun culture and it is the target of the next two stories: one by Gregory Galloway, the other by Ron Koertge. Gregory offers a realistic look at hunting with an unexpected turn in which the target becomes something unexpected and outrageous. Ron's fable offers a clever twist on a familiar trope. In this one, two deer, normally the prey, decide to turn the tables by hiring a human bodyguard!

Alex Flinn's story that follows is a provocative look at a gun-loving family that defies stereotypes and comes to have a . . . well, *unusual* but crucial reason for valuing their firearms.

Chris Lynch then presents an offbeat love story, which combines affection for a new bride with that for a brace of pistols. It proves to be an uneasy mix.

Eric Shanower's satirical graphic story is also about love, contemplating what happens when Cupid is persuaded to trade in his arrows for something more deadly.

The tragedy of school shootings has become emblematic of our time and is examined in the next two stories by Francesca Lia Block and Jenny Hubbard. Francesca's is narrated by a caring teacher whose classroom has been invaded, while in Jenny's story it is a student who is the narrator, recalling a senseless tragedy that befell a favorite teacher.

It's important to remember that gun violence is hardly a new thing nor is it confined to the United States, as Elizabeth Wein depicts in a story set in Scotland during World War II.

Edward Averett's moodily evocative tale reveals the inner workings of a disturbed boy's mind and its impact on his strong-willed grandmother, while the two final stories, by Peter Johnson and Joyce Carol Oates, thoughtfully examine, in their individual ways, the juxtaposition of guns and unintended consequences.

So there you have it, fourteen original pieces by sixteen celebrated authors, all examining aspects of guns and gun culture. Will they change your mind about the issue or will they reinforce your existing opinions? Read them and find out.

TAKING AIM

POWER AND PAIN, TEENS AND GUNS

A CULTURE OF GUNS...
WITH COMMENTS FROM SONS

Marc Aronson, Will Weaver, Chris Crutcher

Marc Aronson

Preface: The other day my two sons, ages fourteen and nine, realized that their elaborate water guns were broken and so bought Nerf guns to while away hot summer days in our suburban town. Since then I see them standing in the kitchen, by the front door, locked and loaded—menacing and ready to shoot.

Shooting itself is more of a problem, as the darts are very easy to lose—so, for now, the guns are for posing.

Neither of my sons has ever been closer to a real gun than when they have passed a policeman or seen guards at an airport. But they know the stance—taken from TV, games, YouTube, movies—and they know how guns are meant to make you look: masculine, tough, ready, dangerous, not to be messed with.

I was just like my sons when I was growing up in Manhattan: my parents once brought home a prop from a show: a supposedly Revolutionary War rifle, but empty of all the workings. I kept it proudly in my closet to show friends, and to pretend shoot. Once, at camp, out in the California scrub brush, I took a shot with a Daisy air rifle (I saw their advertisements all of the time in my comic books).

I stumbled, the shot went who knows where, and I gave up on being a rifleman. *The Rifleman* was a popular TV show at the time and even produced books for readers my age; Chuck Connors, the lantern-jawed hero, enjoyed the distinction of having played both professional basketball and baseball and was even drafted by a pro football team. In 1962 when I was twelve, Chuck and his rifle was one clear image of being a man. But as I learned with my shot, that was not who I was going to be.

One of my classmates had a different image of manhood: he wanted to be a marine. We played at being the toughest of tough soldiers, watched war movies, savored the thought of battling through the kind of relentless boot camp that would make you a man. Of course we'd be armed. It didn't turn out that way. Ours was the "High School of Vietnam Protests"—if we heard anything about guns it was rumors of armed revolutionary Black Panthers. Guns faded entirely out of my life.

THE QUESTION

What are guns for? Where do they fit in our society? There is a big answer and many smaller answers. The big answer is that we in America think of ourselves as a nation where the individual can "make it." We each have the chance to improve ourselves, but we must do that alone. According to that image of America, we, or our forebearers, chose to come, found a way to survive, and where we go from here is up to us. A gun is to each one of us like a crown and scepter is to a king—it is that power that stands for what we each can do alone: hunt for game, protect our homes, fight for our country. Beliefs like this have resulted in America having by far the highest gun ownership rate in the world: eighty-eight guns for every hundred people.

Gun = personal power. For men, of course, a gun means you are potent, virile, "big," "well hung" in all of its meanings. And so to take away a man's guns is to castrate him, to turn him from an *hombre*, a power, into a eunuch. That is what I hear in the ferocious opposition to even the mildest gun laws—the sense that to take away a man's guns is to create a nation of flaccid weaklings who can easily be cowed by any greedy and intrusive government. A gun keeps the hungry government at bay—so a man can stand tall and proud. In turn, as some gun owners demand to be allowed to show guns in public—on trains, in the streets, in schools—they are saying: trust no one, give no power to police, lawmen, rules of society— carry heat, stand tall, dare anyone to cross you. Show your guns, show your six-pack, show your hot, hard weapon.

Except, of course, that story is wrong. Some of us were here already when the northern Europeans came: Native Americans, Spanish in the Southwest, French from the north down along the Ohio and Mississippi Rivers. Some of us did not choose to come here—enslaved Africans. So coming here was not just about individuals; it depended on which group you belonged to. And guns—if you had them—have always been regulated.

Yes, most Americans in colonial days had guns for hunting—but many of those weapons were not terribly efficient, such that by the time of the Revolution, militias were told to bring only military-grade muskets. (This history is explored in a well-crafted podcast: http://backstoryradio.org/shows/straight-shot-guns-in-america-2/.) The Second Amendment to the Constitution, beloved of gun fanciers, actually states that: "A well-regulated Militia, being necessary to the security of a free State, the right of the people to keep and bear Arms, shall not be infringed." In other words, the purpose of protecting the right for citizens to have guns is to provide for a "well-regulated" force in service to the state—not random individuals standing against the government. Similarly out in the Wild West, it made sense to carry a gun when you were out alone in vast spaces with no way to get help. But the towns of the West, such as Dodge City and Tombstone, required you to check your guns—to put them aside. After the Civil War, one of the missions of groups such as the Ku Klux Klan was to take guns away from African Americans.

While there is one grand image of guns in America—I am Packing, I am Strong—in fact what a gun has meant to Americans has depended entirely on which kind of American you were: where you lived, what your neighbors thought of you. There are different gun stories throughout America. My older son, he of the Nerf poses, said to me that guns are like cars: they seem really cool and powerful, but they are murder unless you know how to use them. And, I suspect, none of us in our family will ever get that training.

So, to shift from images of masculinity and history lessons to real experience, I asked author Will Weaver, who lives in northern Minnesota and happened to be traveling in Alaska with one of his sons, to describe guns in his America. I live with Nerfs and TV images—what do guns mean out his way?

Will Weaver

When my son was about seven years old, we had "the talk." Not about sex, but about guns. Certainly he had seen them around our house. Long guns—shotguns and rifles—for hunting, usually cased unless I was cleaning them after a pheasant-hunting trip to South Dakota, or after grouse or deer hunting in northern Minnesota where we live. Guns coming and going during the fall season, then put away. And he had his own BB gun, a Daisy-brand lever action that I had bought for him on his fifth birthday. But now that he was bigger, it was time for the "guns are not toys" talk.

"I thought it was going to be about girls," he would say later, and we had a good laugh about that.

Later, in this case, is now. Owen is suddenly thirty, a tall, slim, bearded guy with bright blue eyes who lives in Brooklyn, and we are spending a week of time together in Alaska, where he has a rare week off from his life as a professional musician. I've flown up from Minnesota to hang out with him and do some fishing, but it's raining steadily, thrumming on the metal roof of our rental cabin, and we're happy to be going nowhere today. We're just talking. Getting caught up.

In Alaska, as in Minnesota, the conversation often includes guns in natural and innocuous ways. One of the musical event producers here on the Kenai Peninsula was worried about the New Yorkers and their safety, and had given Owen and his music ensemble the "bear talk."

"'If you're hiking, stick together. Watch for bears if there are salmon in the creek. And never get between a sow and her cubs,'" Owen says, mimicking an "I'm talking to idiots" voice. But then he smiled. "The guy also said, 'You should always carry a gun—or at least, bear spray.'" He laughs. "I wanted to say, 'Hey, I live in Bed-Stuy—I'm always packing heat.'"

Though with my son, nothing could be further from the truth. While he grew up around guns, he's not a gun guy in any way. I seize the moment to tell him about this book I'm involved with, one with other writers, in which we are trying to talk about guns in America. Trying to make some sense of their place in our national life.

He stretches out on the lumpy couch, puts his hands behind his head. "My first memory of guns is shooting my BB gun at pop cans," he muses. "That 'plinking' sound. It was fun. Then we moved up to a .22 rifle—which you made sure to tell me 'was not a toy.' You had me shoot a ripe tomato. I was really surprised at how it blew apart."

I nod.

"Good parenting there, Pops," he says with a sideways look. "Entrance hole, exit hole—very different things. That exploding tomato stuck with me."

"Good."

"Oh—and then that watermelon, the one you shot with your shotgun? I remember that you drew a face on it."

I shrug. "Maybe I was being too obvious."

"Obvious is a good thing with gun-safety training," he said. And from there we meandered down the family memory lane—the one of guns and hunting. Or not hunting, in Owen's case, which was an earthquake to the male side of my family.

"Dead animals' pictures," as my wife calls them, constitute about 50 percent of the photos of my youth. Ditto with my father's and grandfather's old photos. Endless hunting pictures confirmed by taxidermy about the house: deer heads hung on the wall; a mottled partridge perched atop a bookcase; a fluffy coyote hide draping the back of my father's couch; a beaver-pelt rug. But I saw early signs that Owen was not going to carry on this tradition.

Once, when he was four or five years old, I came home from duck hunting and proudly presented two fine green head mallards. Owen stared at them. "Don't ducks have rights?"

It was a watershed moment, one that has become family lore for a great laugh. He was not trying to be a smart aleck or sarcastic; it was his truth at that very moment, and I was lucky to recognize it as such.

As he grew into middle school, he went hunting with me, though reluctantly and not often, much to the dismay of his grandfather. I found myself making excuses—that Owen had basketball practice, that he had to study, that he was spending time with his girlfriend—and so he couldn't go hunting. My father, in a last-ditch effort, bought Owen a brand-new, high-powered deer rifle, a fine Remington .243 with a telescopic sight, and inked his name on the leather case. But Owen has never shot that rifle, either at a target or a deer, and probably never will. It was a difficult time in our family, back then, but we got through it and out the other side. And maybe my family's struggles with the role of guns is a small-scale model of our American family's dilemma: What are we to do about guns in America?

As the rain continued that afternoon, we went into town, to Soldotna, to find an internet café. After we got caught up on our email, we wandered next door to a big sporting goods store to look for better rain gear for fishing the next day.

The gun counter area was busy, and we spent some time looking at rifles and shotguns, their heft, their fine craftsmanship, their beauty in some cases. Nearby was the ammunition aisle, a tidy library of bullets in calibers from the lowly .22, to shotgun shells, to .50-caliber hollow-point bullets that would stop a water buffalo. The shelves were fully stocked.

"No hoarding here," I murmur.

In our town of Bemidji, Minnesota, a small city up near the headwaters of the Mississippi River, the ammunition truck comes on Wednesday. I know this, because I recently tried to buy some .22 shells, but the sporting goods store (a national chain) was out of stock. For certain calibers, the shelves were bare or nearly so.

"Gotta get here on Wednesday when the truck comes," the clerk told me.

I waited for more explanation.

"It's the ammo hoarders," he explained, lowering his voice. He gave a shrug of helplessness. "They think Obama's gonna take away their guns, so they keep stocking up on ammo."

I laugh. The clerk doesn't.

"Wednesday," he says flatly, "or Friday at the latest," and turns away.

Owen can only shake his head at the story, and we leave the gun section.

On our way to the front, we pass by a display of toy guns. They include a replica .45-caliber water pistol; a soft dart–type toy machine gun with a curving, banana clip; a "zombie hunter" pellet gun; a "special forces/SWAT" paintball gun; and pink guns for little girls. All of them have the orange "this is a toy gun" muzzle marker, but they look easy to remove.

Owen picks up a toy M16 assault air rifle with laser/tactical grip. Compared to hunting rifles and shotguns with their smooth curves, it's an ugly, misshapen cousin. Its design is for war. For killing.

"Isn't this the kind school shooters like to use?" he asks.

"Among others," I reply.

Owen shivers. "We're sort of screwed," he says softly as he puts the toy gun back in its place. "This country, I mean."

I pause. One part of me, my secret, pessimistic mind, agrees with him: there's no answer to gun violence in

America. That things have to get worse—way worse before they get better. That we have to hit bottom, and that "bottom" is not even close.

But there's another voice in me, the part that believes we have to be optimistic; the part that tries, even now, to be the good and cheerful parent. "At some point, we'll get it right," I say. "At some point, this country will figure it out. We always do, eventually."

He gives me a sidelong look, wry and knowing, that says he understands what I'm up to. But he doesn't call me out on it.

"Come on, Pops," he says. "Let's get out of here. I'll buy you a coffee."

Chris Crutcher

When I'm talking with students about the differences between now and when I went to high school, something I always mention is our lettermen's club fund-raiser, during which we raised money for an entire year's activities. We auctioned off a shotgun. And we presented it to the winner *in school*. These days, a kid walks down the hall with a shotgun, he or she gets a trip to juvie—minimum. a psych evaluation.

If the winner of that shotgun—and it was usually a guy—were to put it where it *belonged*, it would be in the gun rack of his unlocked pickup, and that pickup wouldn't look a lot different from the six or seven other pickups in the lot except more than likely the guns in *those* racks would be deer rifles.

Another difference between then and now is that the likelihood of that student bringing the gun *back into the school* for purposes of malice was almost zero. I'm not saying there were no shootings, but the kind of mayhem that occurred at Columbine or Virginia Tech or Aurora or Newtown was nearly impossible because nobody had the firepower to pull it off. In the Idaho gun culture where I grew up, it was pretty much unthinkable to *allow* citizens to own that kind of destructive force.

It was unthinkable because it was stupid. And it still is.

I learned a long time ago debating politics with my father that if you allow your opponent to start the conversation with a faulty basic premise, you've lost before it begins. That guns equal freedom is a faulty basic premise. The gun nuts—I call them "gnuts"; the *g* is silent—would have us believe that the framers of the Constitution wanted us to have as many guns as we desire with huge clips and cop-killer ammo to keep our government from becoming tyrannical. Not only did none of that paraphernalia exist when the Constitution was drafted, but our government, be it Democrat or Republican, is not in danger of becoming that. The NRA is tyrannical; the government is not. And besides, our government has drones. It has bunker-buster bombs. It has nuclear warheads. We're not allowed to have any of those things, so in the war against supposed tyranny, it would be: government: 1, gnuts: 0.

I tend to agree with Will Weaver's son (whom I'm considering adopting) that we've gone way too zany in this argument to ever become rational again. The entire male gnut population gets an erection because Sarah Palin (claims to) shoot wolves from the air. Vladimir Putin goes all anti-American and sales of AK47s shoot through the roof (pun intended) because, I mean, what if Russia cuts us off? How can we protect our families without our AKs? Folks, if that nighttime murderer/hostage-taker, who statistically will *never* enter your house, does in fact enter your house, you're as likely to take out members of your family as you are this Freddy Krueger–esque menace when you start firing at his shadow with a machine gun. I know, I know, it's not technically a machine gun, but tell that to the parents of the Newtown kids, or the Aurora moviegoers.

I recently lost the friendship of a fellow author when he took issue with some (one of many) unkind thing I said on my Facebook page about Ted Nugent, the gnut has-been rocker who keeps himself in the public eye with his astonishing insensitivity. My author friend was trying to make a case that Ted is really a bleeding-heart softie who quietly finds ways to feed hungry children at the same time he leads the charge to save the planet. I have no idea if those things are true, and I don't care because I can find plenty of children-savers who don't publicly taunt the parents and loved ones of victims of senseless gun violence. When enough of my Facebook followers had messaged me to "dump that ignorant a-hole" from my Facebook conversation, I deleted it because I didn't want people thinking he was an ignorant a-hole. He abruptly accused me of censorship. File that under "No Good Deed Goes Unpunished." Had the conversation gone on, I would have said I don't care what Ted Nugent does privately, because he's a public figure who arouses legions of lazy thinkers into believing they can look smart and tough uttering sound bites from the NRA, delivered to us through Fox Entertainment.

I have another close friend, who is still a *close* friend, who frequently takes a boat into international waters. He owns an AR15 because he wants to be able to stand with it on the bow of his boat to deter pirates, should any decide they want what he has. Though I would eagerly bet a million dollars that he will never have occasion to hoist that lethal apparatus to ward off hungry bad guys, to some degree his thinking makes sense. Just ask Captain Phillips. But here's my question for that friend: If you knew that giving up that weapon, and the right to own that weapon, would bring back the five- and six-year-olds in Newtown, or the moviegoers in Aurora, or the college students at Virginia Tech, or the hundreds and hundreds of poverty-stricken kids who fall on our city streets each year, would you make that sacrifice?

See, I don't want my friend's gun. I don't want my ex-friend-author's guns. Hell, I don't even want Ted Nugent's guns. I know the first two are safe owners and there probably isn't a safer gun owner in the world than Ted Nugent. Ted knows if *any* bad thing happened with a gun that could be traced back to him, the entire Fox Entertainment staff would desert him like a pack of lemmings.

I don't want their guns. I want their votes.

It will take at least a generation—maybe two—from the day we start, for the United States to get sane about guns again. Conventional wisdom changes slowly, and conventional wisdom will have to come around to the conclusion that the magnitude of your firepower has nothing to do with the magnitude of your penis.

I get it about hunting, though I don't hunt. I get it about protection, though I've never believed I needed a gun to protect myself and have never been in a situation where I did. Even the most outrageous antigun liberals haven't focused on hunting rifles or that handgun kept at the ready in a high-crime-area convenience store, or secured safely away from children in a home. At this point, we're asking for *background checks* for crying out loud; an exercise, by the way, that wouldn't have filtered out most of our famous school or workplace shooters because they didn't have a background until they created it with their first mass murder.

I marvel at the gnuts who say, "This isn't about guns, it's about *mental health*." I was in the mental health business in one way or another for thirty years, and one *certainty* is that politicians who spew the same drivel as the gnuts would be far less likely to vote for the cost of the legislation it would take to bring our mental health system to a point at which it could be helpful with this issue than they would be to provide sane gun legislation. *Plus*, sane mental health legislation and gun legislation are not mutually exclusive. To address this particular issue, they belong hand in hand. Meantime, though we don't know who the next shooter will be, we know what he'll use.

Folks, guns have one purpose. They put holes in things, and what is in those things leaks out. So often, that thing is life.

ROACH

Walter Dean Myers

I wake up in a state of sheer panic. My hands are shaking, as I struggle to catch my breath. I can feel the wetness of my pillow and I want to move but all I can manage is to clench my jaw tighter. My eyes are wide open and it seems I can see everything in the room at the same time. It is all in black and dark grays and spinning crazily around me. I try to locate myself and finally see my dresser against the wall where it should be. Closing my eyes, I turn my head so I can face the mirror. I slide my elbow slowly along the sheet, trying to sense if the skin on my arm is still smooth. I raise my shoulders and look at the image in the mirror. My face, dark brown, the whites of my eyes reflecting the morning light, my mouth slightly open, everything is as it should be. If I had really changed, I would have seen it.

My legs are stiff and slightly sore as I move them over the side of the bed and turn toward the mirror. It is still me, Gregory Walls, wide-eyed and staring from the bed.

I glance down at my hands and flex my fingers. They are all right, too.

A knock on the door. It would be my mother; Gertie would have come right in.

"You okay?" she asks. "I heard you calling out."

"I'm okay," I say, breathing through my open mouth, trying to remember myself calling out.

"You want something to eat?"

"No," I lie.

I look at the clock. A quarter to seven.

I hear my mother's heavy footsteps as she moves away from the door. Instantly my mind is filled with the same image that had awakened me. I am scurrying across the linoleum floor, wondering how I have become so small, when I catch a glimpse of myself in one of the empty soda bottles that my sister has lined up for recycling day. For a second I am frozen. In the reflection of the empty bottle my image is somewhat distorted, but there is no question that I am a roach. It is the second time I have had the dream, although the thought seems somehow to have slipped into my waking hours, and occasionally I catch myself looking away from mirrors, afraid of what I might see.

There is moisture in the cold air. Not enough for it to be raining, but enough so that the tires of the trucks that pass in the street below are hissing. A garbage truck stops and announces its presence as workers bang the metal cans against it. From beyond the door drifts the scent of bacon and I imagine my mother standing in front of the stove. Gertie will already be at the kitchen table, her elbows on either side of her plate, waiting for her breakfast. I imagine her thinking about me. Sometimes it's as if she has secrets buried deep within her brain, visions that she keeps to herself. Over the summer, when she lost her baby she wept for weeks, but then, suddenly, got over it. Now she stays home and keeps the house in order. She does a good job at it. Sometimes I think she cares for me the way she would have cared for a baby.

When I first told Gertie that I felt that my body was changing, she asked me how it was changing. A natural question, but one I couldn't answer. She opened my shirt to take a closer look. We are close, my sister and I. We have always looked after each other.

"You're okay," she said, buttoning my shirt. "You're just tired."

Tired, yes.

Gertie had brought my breakfast to the bed as I knew she would. Mama didn't want to deal with me anymore. That was her way. When things went badly in one direction, she would simply go in another—our things in shopping bags and suitcases and boxes as we moved to a different apartment. Sometimes she would find a different man, sometimes a different job, but it was always the same. Us wandering through the city trying to find a place that seemed right.

I am standing in front of the mirror again. Staring, looking for changes. Out of the corner of my eye, I see the door crack and Gertie looking at me. I smile at her as she comes into the room, her arms behind her back.

"I'm going to school today," I say.

"You had that meeting yesterday?" she asks. "I know Mama went with you yesterday. What did they say?"

"A lot of stuff about what I need to be doing with my life," I say. "Same old, same old."

"You going to be all right?"

"Yeah, sure."

No, I think. *Can't you see I'm changing?*

She smiles and leaves my room.

There is a roach crawling on the wall. It is going straight up at first, then stops and veers sharply right for a few inches, and then straight up again. Where is it going? What signals it to change directions? I pick up a shoe and know I can end its life with one jump and a swing of the shoe. Instead I watch it crawl to the ceiling and then disappear over the wooden molding.

Down the stairs. I am so nervous. The hallway smells of urine and garbage. There are radios playing behind the closed doors and a variety of cooking smells. A door opens on the second floor and closes quickly as I pass.

On the street. It is spring warm, with a few raindrops that hit my face and hands. I stuff my hands quickly into my pockets.

The corner of 145th Street. There is a huddle of gray-and-black-clad figures on the corner, all wearing hoodies or do-rags; some have backpacks. They collect themselves on the corner as they do every day, huddling together, hoods covering their heads, their faces, reducing them to a horde of gray shadows. I stop and stare as one figure, moving in small, quick steps between the others, looks like a roach standing on its back legs. I am breathing heavily again. Cold sweat drips down my side and I remember the therapist talking about "anxiety" attacks.

"They happen when you imagine that something dreadful will happen even though it's not logical," the school psychologist said. She comes to our school twice a month. "You have to ask yourself if it's at all reasonable to imagine what is in your mind."

I tell myself that the very thought of these people being roaches is nonsense. It was a stupid thought, I say, but one that I know will come back again. I stop on the corner of Fred Douglass Boulevard and look back. What am I looking for?

Drifting across the street, I move toward Bradhurst ahead of some of them.

"Greg, where you going?" Tyrone startles me.

"School," I say. "Guess I got to put some time in."

"I hear that," Tyrone comes back. "You want to go to Brooklyn?"

I wonder if kids in Brooklyn say they are going to Harlem when they mean they're going to get high.

"I ain't got no money, Ty," I say.

"I can lay a buzz on you," he answers. His eyes are already glassy as he scans the nabe. "What's today, Tuesday? Got to get nice to face a Tuesday, G-Man."

"Yeah." We are walking up the hill. Tyrone is talking about colleges he would like to go to. Which ones have the sweetest honeys. Fantasy.

He and I have been homeboys since back in the day. We used to make plans about what we were going to be and how we were going to conquer the world. Back in the day.

We go around to the windows of the boys' bathroom, and Ty hands his backpack through a window to avoid security.

In school, through the metal detectors, past the cop on the desk, down the hall to the boys' bathroom. Ty gets his backpack, and fishes out some weed. Four dollars a joint and it all went in two minutes.

The first bell rings and there is a scramble to get out to classes.

"Gimme a minute," Ty says, grabbing me by the arm and taking his gear out of his backpack. "I got to get a little taste."

I know he has been using for a while. Still, the slim needle is upsetting and I look away. He hands me his backpack and goes into a stall. I go to the window and look out at the bodega across the street. Two old men hang out in front of the store. I know they were trying to sell lucys—loose cigarettes—to customers before the regular customers went into the bodega to buy them. I think about Ty in the bathroom and wonder what I would do if he nodded out. I start toward the door of the stall, stop, then walk to the sink, put our backpacks on the floor, and start washing my hands.

Suddenly the door to the bathroom opens and the sound of a whistle echoes off the tile walls.

"Yo, man, you didn't hear the first bell ring?" Mr. Sanders, short, fat, brown, and loudmouthed. "What you doing standing in here? Get out to your first class!"

For a split second, I think maybe Sanders won't look into the stalls.

Wham! He kicks the first one open as I scoop the backpacks up and leave the bathroom.

I can hear the second door being kicked and know Ty is busted. I walk down the hall and stand in front of one of the girl's lockers, my hands shaking. A moment later,

Sanders is bringing Ty out. He has him by the shoulder and has one hand twisted behind his back. Ty's left sleeve is rolled up and I know he was on a nod.

Everybody looking. Everybody talking. Kids scattering in every direction moving away from Sanders in his glory. He has caught a kid shooting up.

"First class! First class!" Pushing Ty down the hall. "Y'all heard the bell ring!"

I don't have to look at his face to know he is smiling. We are animals to him, insects.

English. I am sitting in the back of the class. The teacher, Miss Lapides, is droning on about Christopher Marlowe, how he was killed in a bar in London and what a shame it all was.

"Life wasn't easy in Marlowe's day, and there were bad neighborhoods in London as well as any other place," she is saying.

I tune her out and begin thinking about Ty. The good thing is that they won't be able to charge him with selling. Selling brings a heavy bid and I am sure he had left his stuff in his backpack.

"And Marlowe was only twenty-nine when he was

killed! Can you imagine that!" Miss Lapides says.

"He was old," a girl says. "He should have been living in Harlem! He might not have lasted that long."

Only Miss Lapides wasn't laughing.

Miss Lapides is at her desk. She is reading from some play that Marlowe wrote. No one in the class is interested. Under the desk I am going through Ty's bag. There is a plastic bag full of pill bottles, maybe seven or eight. There is a book—*The Watsons Go to Birmingham*—and a gun. It is small as I lay it in the palm of my hand.

Bells ring. I am in the gym. There is a basketball practice and some guys from the school team are running five-on-four drills. They are quick, darting up and down the floor as the ball goes magically through them. They all look the same, dark and thin, with legs that move crazily across the polished wooden floor. The squeaking of their sneakers is background to the casual conversations of the non-ballplayers. I watch as a skinny arm reaches over the rim to stop a shot. Can real people do that?

Then the door opens and three cops, one in plain clothes, come into the gym with Ty. I freak out for a moment because I think they are looking for the backpack I'm sitting on. But they just take Ty across the floor and out through the gym doors. His face is puffed and they force his head down as they half carry, half drag him through the gym and out of the doors. Some dudes look out the window and count that there are three squad cars waiting to take Ty away.

"Why didn't they take him out the front door?" a boy asks.

Shrugs. I know they wanted us to see him. *Look, we don't respect him or any of you,* they are saying. We all know that.

I imagine myself being dragged out of the school or maybe just surrounded by the cops. A flicker of a movie runs through my head. They don't draw their weapons even though I am holding Ty's gun in my hand. Instead they pull out cans of roach spray. I push away the image. Into a corner of my mind. With the others.

The buzz is about Ty, and lies about his being arrested bounce around the gym like a volleyball. One of the ball-players calls Ty a chump and the others join in. What do they see when they see themselves? They run and jump so someone gives them a ball and calls them "athletes." What does Ty do? He scurries in the darkness of his own soul, and someone gives him a needle and some dope and calls him a "junkie." It is a roach circus with different props.

I feel slightly nauseous.

On the way home. I'm hating on the ballplayers and it feels good, but I can't find a reason to hang on to the moment. It is just that they are wrong to dis Ty. They are wrong, thinking they are better than Ty, wrong to think their skills move them to a different level. We are all the same.

Home. Lying on the bed. The backpack is on the floor in the corner, but I have taken the gun out and it is under the pillow. It comforts me. When my mother comes into the room, she stops at the foot of the bed, turns slightly, and gives me her over-the-shoulder look.

"You didn't go to school today?" she accuses me with the question.

"I went."

She gives me a look that says she doesn't believe me. I give her a look back as if I don't give a shit if she believes me or not. She closes the door hard as she leaves.

I stretch out across the bed, looking at nothing, trying not to think about anything, wondering if I should call Ty's mom. She had to know what happened, that he had been arrested, taken out of school. If all they found were his works, maybe he could cop a plea and get a bench date or a couple of weeks in juvie.

Corner of my eye. A movement. A roach on the dresser. I see it and then I don't. Where has it gone? Does it think that this is its room? Its world?

Gertie at the door. Tyrone is on her phone. She tosses it to me.

"Yo, what's up?" I ask as Gertie sits on the bed.

"Hey, man, I'm calling from the slam," Tyrone says. "You feeling me?"

"Yeah." I know the phone call would be monitored.

"You got my stuff?"

"Yeah."

"Look, I need to get the snacks to Blue down at the Spot," Tyrone says. In the background, I can hear somebody yelling in Spanish. "My bail is two benjamins, and that's right on time, you got me?"

"Yeah."

"And hold on to everything else," Ty goes on. "I'll tighten you up when I'm back in the world. You gonna take care of business for me?"

"No problem," I say.

"Peace out, bro."

"Peace out."

Ty hangs up. Gertie looks at me, wondering why Ty is in jail. I tell her he got busted in school for using dope.

She doesn't speak but her head is down and I know she is worried about me. I don't want the conversation that is going through her head so I head it off by turning on the television.

On the screen there are a man and a woman. He is white, she is either light-skinned black or Spanish, and they are making light jokes about the news. They are pretty, handsome, so far from anything I know that is real. I change the channel.

There are two women looking at a vacuum cleaner they claim is really marvelous and picks up hidden dirt. The apartment they live in is spotless and only the vacuum cleaner can find that hidden dirt.

Gertie reaches over and takes the remote from me. She turns off the television.

She wears her innocence like a veil you can't quite see through. When she wants, she can open me with a smile and make me show her everything I am thinking and feeling.

"You got to be careful," she says. "People can't tell who is who. You get around dope people and all they see is . . ." She shrugs.

"Yo, Gertie, I ain't tripping into no dope," I say. "I'm strong as the day is long."

She tilts her head back and to one side and nods slightly. She smiles. I smile back. She pats my hand gently before leaving. She is my salvation, my truth. But when she leaves, I check out the mirror again, and the mirror is dropping nothing but truth.

You're holding your looks together, but you know who you are.

I am wounded bad and the tears come down my face. It's how roaches bleed. I need to move, to get up and work on some geography before I get fixed to the bed.

The Spot is all the way downtown: 126th Street and St. Nicholas. I don't want to deal with Ty but I don't want to leave him in the wind, either. If Ty is saying that he is looking for two benjamins, I know the stuff in the vial is either Girl or some jerky prescription stuff. It is something to do, get the money and give it to his mother so she can bail him out.

Walk downtown. Just don't cross 135th near the

station because too many cops hang out there. They'll stop and put you against the wall just to pass the time of day. I tuck the drugs around my laptop, and the gun in my jacket pocket. The gun makes me feel better, makes me feel less like something that can just be stepped on.

Down St. Nicholas. People walking the street, they check me out and I see some of them turn away. What do they see?

"Hey, Greg, what happened to your man today?" Two ballplayers from school.

"You saw what happened," I say as one steps in front of me.

"I heard he was selling weed in the bathroom," Ballplayer says. He is smiling. From his height he looks down on me, even leans back a little to make sure I notice.

I start to step around him and he puts his fingers on my chest. "He's bringing the school down with his foul ass!" Ballplayer says.

The words come out: *He's bringing the school down with his foul ass!* But they mean something different: *You and your boy ain't nothing! You're roaches we can step on!*

More words come to add to the pile. I think about the gun but his words stop. I move on.

I think about the roach on my wall. If I had jumped with my shoe, I could have flattened it against my wall. It would have been so quick the roach wouldn't have been able to distinguish between living and dying.

But if the roach had had a gun . . . Stupid thought. It wouldn't be a roach if it had a gun.

"You have to ask yourself if it's at all reasonable to imagine what is in your mind."

The Spot. Gray, plain, the bricks have been painted over dozens of times. On the left side of the door, someone has drawn a crude eye with three tears under it. Three dudes dead in the building. Not bad for a place like this. Four steps into the vestibule where two guys play chess on a wooden box. The bald one wears a Sacramento Kings T-shirt, and the other one has dirty-looking dreads over a wife beater. A radio on the floor spits some stupid rap as the two guys pretend not to notice me standing there.

"I came to see Blue," I say.

"Who's that?" Baldy says, not looking up. "I don't know no Blue."

"Guy sent me here with his stuff," I say.

"Let me see it."

"Uh-uhn."

"Then you can't get in."

"Okay, just tell him I was here," I say, turning away.

"Hey, second floor, apartment fourteen."

They look me up and down as I step past the narrow opening they give me. I see the machete leaning against the wall.

Upstairs. The hall is dark and it takes me a while to see. Good. A roach would see in the dark and smell where the people are. I am not a roach. I find 14 and knock. The peephole clicks, lets a red light flash through for a second and closes. The door opens and I hear music. A girl is at the door, small, skinny, shiny eyes.

"Hey, baby," she slurs.

"Where's Blue?"

She points to a room and I go toward it. On a couch in the hallway leading to the room there is a guy hunched over, his arms across his body, his head on his knees. I stop and watch for a second until I see him breathe. I take another step and look in. There are mattresses on the floor and people lying on them. They are either high or dead. This is the Spot, so I think high. In one corner of the room, there is a mound of black flesh sitting in a high-back chair. Blue. Everybody knows his ugly ass. He is big even when he is sitting. He's holding a magazine up to the light creeping through the dirty blinds. There are other people in the room on the floor. In the red light, I can barely make out their forms. The stink pushes at me as I stand in the middle of the floor.

"What you want?" he grunts. Uptown they say he killed his own brother over ten dollars. Roach talk.

"You know Tyrone?"

"Schoolboy, I know him." He grunts his words. "What you want?"

"He told me to bring you some stuff," I say.

"Turn the light on," he says. "It's near the door."

I find the light switch and flip it up. For a moment I think everyone will jump up and start running around. Nobody moves.

"Let me see the stuff." This from Blue.

I take the stuff out of my pocket and show it to Blue. "Ty said two benjamins."

"Why he didn't bring the shit himself?" Blue opens a plastic bottle and sniffs it.

"He's busy," I say.

"Fifty cents is all I can do," Blue says. "This ain't nothing but some watered-down crap."

"I'll take it back," I say. "He doesn't need fifty cents, he needs—"

"Don't be telling me what you going to do." Blue is on his feet. When he moves toward me, letting his bulk push me back, it is like we are doing theater. He is huge and I am small, and I am supposed to tremble and he is supposed to have his way with me, to step on what is left of Gregory, of who I had been or what Gertie called me. He is on me in a flash and can transform me from living to dead before I even know it, before I can scurry away to some dark hole.

A fat hand around my neck, leaning against me so that his sweaty brow touches my face, sending signals of all the bad things he can do to me through my wavering antennae and down to my trembling heart. He is Blue and I am just another roach, like the ones lying on the floor around him, like the ones in the hallway, like Ty, like the ballplayers who think they are special.

Blue is so sure of himself, so full of his power that he does not feel me pulling the gun from my pocket. Even when the gun goes off, when the sound, muffled by his rolls of fat, explodes with a loud *poof* into his body, he is still holding my neck. I pull the trigger again and again and he falls back.

A frozen moment. Blue is standing three feet away from me, trying to figure out what has happened. He starts to sag and reaches up to grab some invisible bar, then sinks to the floor, slowly at first and then faster as his weight carries him backward.

A girl, maybe the one who opened the door, rushes toward Blue. I think she is going to try to help him but she is reaching into his shirt. She pulls out a brown paper bag, tears it open, and money tumbles to the floor. She grabs as much as she can and heads toward the door.

I think about Ty. I take some of the money, trying not to look at it, and then I start out of the room, flipping the light out as I leave. Behind me, someone is speaking. A crackhead trying to come out of his stupor, wondering what has happened.

I am down the stairs. The chess players are on their feet looking down the street.

"Something must have happened up there!" Dreads is saying as I push past him.

There is no story in the papers. The streets whisper about Blue being killed at the Spot but they get it wrong. They say that Mookie Duke, a Jamaican player, killed him to get his turf. It doesn't matter that it is all wrong. Mookie Duke is cruising down the Ave taking credit and showing his gold teeth. The street says that he even showed up at Blue's funeral with his crew and laid a rose on Blue's chest. Mookie Duke is the boss now, but who can tell the difference? When the lights come on, we all scurry for the darkness we know. There is no need to think about what has become instinctive.

Ty is back in the world, bragging about his junior bid, and asks me what happened. I say I don't know but that I have done him a solid by copping the two benjamins and want to keep the gun.

"No problem," he says, laughing. "What we got on this reservation is drugs and guns."

I laugh.

I stop going to school and just hustle where I find a spot, sometimes working in the dry cleaners, sometimes sweeping sidewalks. Mom knows it but she doesn't speak on it, which is cool, because she knows there's nothing she can do about it. I don't worry about Blue because he wasn't worth the worrying, but I lay low. The gun makes me feel better. No one is going to jump up with a sneaker and splat my life out against some wall. A gun makes you feel less like a roach.

Sometimes I don't even go home, just find some other hole to lay up in, some shadow to call my spot from time to time. I come out when I'm hungry and there's not too many people around. When I'm needing somebody to hold on to, when I'm needing to get in touch with the Gregory I used to be, I go to see Gertie. I look at her close and she is wondering what it is that I am looking at. I tell her how pretty she is and she is embarrassed. I want to say how human she is, but I don't want to go there in case she doesn't feel the same way about herself. No, I don't want to go there.

EMBRACED BY RAVEN ARMS

Tim Wynne-Jones

The vehicle was backed up to the front porch, the same way the FedEx guy did when he made a delivery. But this wasn't any courier. The van was mud splashed and rusted out, the left bumper bashed in, the back doors wide open.

Morley Bendix held his glasses in place with a finger on the bridge of his nose. They were broken again. The front door of the house opened and he watched their brand-new flat-screen television walk out and down the steps on a pair of bandy legs. Whoever was carrying that thing was so small his head didn't appear above the set. Morley stepped quickly out of sight behind a big maple.

The guy disappeared into the back of the van and was out again and up the steps in no time, tucking in the back of his T-shirt. He stopped at the front door and swiveled around at the waist as if he'd heard the low grunt of shock from thirty yards away. Morley leaned hard into the tree, held his breath, didn't dare peek again until he heard the front door close.

He knew what this was.

It had happened to the Kirkwoods a few months earlier and several other families along lonely River Valley Road. They were sitting ducks out here. These guys just took the easy stuff—hit-and-run. In and out and gone.

Morley knew what to do. He sloughed off his backpack and reached for the cell phone in his pocket, before remembering that his cell phone had disappeared today about the same time he was getting his glasses broken. The rage kicked in, compounded and swelling inside him, and wrapped up inside it—inside the rage—was an idea. It came over him like a wave, electrifying and nauseating in equal parts. Could he do this?

Just don't think, he told himself. *Go!*

Shoving his glasses in his jacket pocket, he took off in long, quiet strides all the way to the garden shed, which he slipped behind just as the front door opened again. A different guy, this one long and gangly with ratty brown hair, carried Mom's iMac. Someone called to him from inside the house. Morley only heard the reply.

"Yeah, yeah, I'll be right there."

The ratty-haired guy delivered the computer to the van and headed back up the stairs.

"Keep your friggin' shirt on," he yelled as he entered the house.

Something too big to carry. Something requiring two pairs of hands. *And there were only two of them.* Even as the door clicked shut, Morley was streaking to the driver's-side door. Unlocked? Of course. And the keys? In the ignition, ready for a quick getaway.

Just way quicker than they expected.

Then just as he was about to slide open the door, there was a loud crash from inside, stopping him cold. He dropped to one knee, his cheek pressed hard against the dirty cold metal of the van. Swearing followed—one of them yelling at the other with the expected volley of curses.

Now!

Morley clambered into the vehicle, tossed his ball cap on the seat, and turned the ignition key. It might have looked like a piece of trash but the engine turned over on the first try and leapt ahead when he tromped on the gas. He went careening down the driveway, things crashing around behind him. He barely stopped to check for traffic on River Valley Road, but it was lightly used and empty now. He slammed on the brakes and the wildly swinging back doors crashed shut. *Yes!* Then he was off again down the hill and up the next, flipping on the lights to cut through the murk and shadows of dusk, until, a quarter mile on, he swung into the Logans' driveway, which was even longer than his own, so that a veil of trees closed behind the stolen van.

Mr. Logan phoned 911 while Mrs. Logan fussed over Morley's bruised face. She thought the thieves had roughed him up. He let her. He tapped his foot anxiously, wanting to get back there—hell, he wanted to run somebody over!

"Let me call your mom," said Mrs. Logan.

"No, it's okay," he said. "I gotta go."

"Not a good idea, son," said Mr. Logan, but the blood was running in Morley and he sloughed off his neighbor's hand.

"The cops should be there by now," he said.

"Even so—"

"It's okay. I'll be careful."

"Leave it to the authorities," Mrs. Logan called after him.

No, he thought. *Nothing gets done when you leave it to the authorities.*

He pulled to a stop on the road outside his own driveway but left the engine running. The doors of the vehicle were all locked; he'd thought of that. He revved the engine, pounded on the steering wheel. Where the hell were they? Then a police cruiser came screaming around the curve up ahead, no siren, no flashing red light—nothing to alert the bad guys. The cruiser swung into the driveway, and Morley followed slowly. The passenger cop stepped out, turned to watch him with his head cocked to one side and his hand on the butt of his holstered gun. Morley stepped out of the van carefully, his hands held high.

"I'm the one who called," he said. "This is my place."

Then he noticed there was someone in the back of the cruiser. He recovered his glasses from his pocket and held them in place. It was Ratty-Hair.

"That's one of them," he said.

The passenger cop nodded, bent to look into the backseat. Ratty slapped the flat of his hand against the window.

"Stupid fuck," said the cop. "He was running down the road, sees us, and takes off into the swamp." He wrinkled his nose. "He's gonna pay for the cleanup job, I'll tell you."

The driver had been on the radio. Now he stepped out of the cruiser.

"You can put your hands down, kid," said the passenger cop, smiling.

Right. Morley rubbed his hands on his thighs, took a deep breath. Ratty smacked the glass again, pointed a finger at him, cocked his thumb, and fired.

They were going to run Ratty in but they wanted the van locked up.

"What about our stuff?"

"Stolen property," said Driver Cop. When they divvied up smiles back at headquarters, Passenger Cop must have taken them all. "It's not just your stuff, kid."

"Yeah, I know," said Morley, hoping the sarcasm in his voice would make his point clear.

"Somebody's got to inventory the whole lot," said Driver Cop, making his own point very clear. *Don't give us any shit, kid.*

"Hey," said Good Cop. "We're doing it by the books, kiddo."

"Right," said Morley, but it wasn't right. It was just one more not-right thing in a not-right day—a not-right day with one shining moment of bravado to make it bearable. The bravado was still humming inside him.

He'd seen this film once where they were running the bulls, some place in Spain—guys racing down the streets with all these longhorns stampeding behind them. That's what he felt like inside. He raked his hands through his hair.

"My hat," he said.

"Huh?"

"It's on the seat."

Driver Cop frowned and gestured toward the van with vaguely concealed annoyance. Right about then, Ratty started pounding on the window of the cruiser and both cops turned to attend to him. Morley opened the driver's door. As he reached across for his baseball cap, a voice said, *"Pssst!"*

He froze. Had there been someone in the van the whole time? His eyes picked out nothing in the shadows—nothing but stolen property.

"Pssst!"

It came again, like air leaking from the seat. He looked down and saw a dark glint, a shining, down the crack of the back of the seat. He dug it out. A gun, its handle covered in lint. A snubby-nosed, little black gun. Before he even knew what he was doing, he'd shoved it in his pocket.

He closed the van door. "Thanks," he said, holding up his hat.

"There'll be someone here in a bit," said Good Cop. "They'll write down what's taken from the vehicle. No biggie."

"Yeah, okay."

"There's a lot of merchandise in there," said Driver Cop, aiming his flashlight through the dirty back windows. "We want to make sure it all gets back to its rightful owner." His voice was testy, distrustful, stressing the word *rightful* as if Morley was a lot closer to *right empty.*

What about quick thinking, kid?

What about thanks for your help?

What about society owes you a debt of gratitude, young man?

Leave it to the authorities.

"Whatever," he said.

Driver Cop looked at him suspiciously in the failing light. "Where'd you get the shiner?"

Morley's hand hovered near his eye, not wanting to touch it. He shrugged.

"Dju have a run-in with these creeps?"

"No, sir."

"You sure?"

He had a look in his eye as if Morley had made the whole thing up. "Happened at school," he said. "Murderball."

Driver Cop didn't nod, wasn't buying it.

"Yeah, well, when you're ready to talk, let us know."

Morley resisted the urge to ask him what had crawled up his ass and died.

"Take it easy, son," said Passenger Cop. "You did good."

You did good.

Morley sat in his bedroom staring at the gun, his

trophy. It was a Raven Arms MP25, semiautomatic. He'd already looked it up on Google: a junk gun, a "Saturday night special," compact and easily concealed. The wooden handle was warmed from holding it. The magazine was empty. No problem. He didn't need bullets, but he did need the gun.

"Hey, Bent-dick."

Morley stopped. Pushed his glasses up his nose. He had given up trying to figure out why Bish Fox hated him.

"You got that money we was talking about?"

Fox sidled in front of him. The busy lunchtime hallway parted like a river around them: Bish, the immovable rock; Morley, the broken stick.

"Yeah," said Morley.

"Good, 'cause I'm sure you're dying to get your cell back." He laughed and poked Morley in the sternum. "Downloaded some great porn. I'll leave it on, no extra charge."

"No, you didn't," said Morley. He couldn't resist. "There's not enough memory."

"Yeah, but I bet you wish I did."

Morley tried to move on, but Bish stopped him with

a hand roughly the size of Morley's chest. "Where you going?"

"I'm not giving you your money here. It'll look like a . . . like a drug transaction."

"A *drug* transaction? Did you really say that? 'A drug trans-*action*.' "

"Not here, okay?"

"Nice try, asshole," said Bish, pressing his hand more firmly.

Time to set the hook.

"Look, I'll meet you," said Morley. "Out by the football field, the equipment locker. Half an hour."

Bishop's hand contracted into a fist, containing in it a hank of Morley's shirt. He knocked on Morley's chest, three times. "Hello," he said. Then he bent down to get right in Morley's bruised face. "You know what happens if you're not there, right?"

"Oh, I . . . yeah. I guess so," said Morley, exhausted by the encounter, rolling his eyes.

"What's that?" said Bish. "You giving me lip?"

Morley sighed, then he grabbed Bishop's fist and threw it off him. "I'll be there!" he snapped, and pushed past the bully. Almost. The fist he'd sloughed off grabbed him by the back of his shirt and yanked him so hard the top button popped off.

"Do not *ever* do that again," whispered Bish in his ear. He held on to Morley's shirt, twisting it in his fist, and Morley cringed, waited, like a dog that had soiled the carpet and was about to get his nose rubbed in it. Then Bish let him go. "Half an hour," he said.

Morley didn't look back. Didn't nod. He would be there, all right.

He didn't know the boy who caught him up a moment later. That is, he'd seen him lurking about but he didn't know his name. One of those nobodies you compare yourself to when you're feeling really, really bad and have to tell yourself that at least you're not that low in the high school caste system. A lurker. A hundred pounds of exposed nerve and bad skin.

"Don't you wish you could kill him?" said the lurker. Morley scowled, but it didn't scare the boy off. "Bishop Fox," said the kid, as if maybe Morley had forgotten the humiliation he'd just been through. "I'm Zane," said lurker-boy, holding out his hand. "Zane Prosser."

Morley didn't take the hand. His mind was elsewhere—out there at the equipment shed already, waiting.

Besides, he didn't want to form an alliance with this weird little dude. Didn't want to touch his hand in case whatever he had was catching.

"I'd kill him if I could," said Zane.

"No, you wouldn't," said Morley.

"I would, too. Him and the others."

Morley stared at the boy. "You'd piss your pants before you got within six feet of him," he said. He hoped hostility would drive the kid off, but Zane only nodded solemnly, as if what he had said was nothing short of true.

"You're right. Once, after he did that to me—what he did to you, back there, shaking me down—I brought a knife to school."

Morley's smile was condescending. "Really?"

"Yeah, I know," said the kid. "You don't believe me. But it's true, I did. I thought of how great it was going to be to shove that knife into him, a hundred different ways."

"That's a lot of ways," said Morley, just for something to say, but he regretted it immediately. It was like an invitation.

"My dad's a hunter, see, so this was one honking big blade. A Ka-Bar. Ever heard of them? It's a combat knife, the ones used by the marines. No kidding. Seven-inch blade, black, very cool. Sharp, too."

"Yeah, and you carried it where? In your lunch pail?"

"Strapped to my leg," said Zane. "I swear. I wanted to use it so bad. Every day I'd think about it. What I'd say to him as I twisted it and twisted it. How he'd scream and beg me to stop."

Morley frowned. The kid looked about twelve, but his eyes looked as if they'd been around a lot longer than the rest of his skinny body.

"You really hate him."

"Damn right," he said. "All of them."

There was that plural again. "All of *them*?"

"You know?" said Zane, his eyes dark and way too serious.

Morley didn't—or he sort of did but he didn't want this little freak thinking they shared anything in common, not even enemies. "I don't know what you're talking about," he said. He said it with disdain—said it the way Bish would have said it to him. Said it as if he was announcing that nothing Zane could say would ever matter to him.

Zane stopped so suddenly, Morley stopped, too, as if they'd come to some invisible red light. The freak glared at Morley, crestfallen. Then his face shut down. Just like that. The lights in his eyes clicked off. But even in the noisy hallway, Morley could hear the kid breathing through his nose, shaky, as if there was a tornado's worth of rage inside him but he'd learned to tamp it way down so that there was nothing of it in his expression, only this sound of air escaping like a pricked balloon followed by the hunger to replace it. He looked to Morley's eyes like a miner trapped under a million tons of coal, waiting in the dark for relief.

Morley moved on, shaking his head, so he didn't see the bitterness in Zane's eyes. Didn't see him mentally add another name to the list in his head.

Morley waited behind the shed. He didn't know what time it was because he didn't have his iPhone. Soon enough he would get it back. He couldn't see Bishop Fox from where he was standing, but he heard him, all right, talking with his cronies fifty yards away at the smoking fence. Bish was holding court, his big voice aimed just that much louder for Morley's benefit. There was laughter. He was making Morley wait. He was getting all the bang for his buck, all he could squeeze out of this latest act of terrorism. The thought made Morley smile to himself.

* * *

And then, there he was, as big as a Coke machine in his red Warrior jacket, which hung open to reveal a gray hoodie with the same Warrior logo on it, a bit of a gut already stretching the fabric. *He's a cliché,* thought Morley. *Does he know he's a cliché?* He'd stay in town, get a job on a road crew or at the 3M plant, if he was lucky. He'd get married and make some woman's life miserable. Meanwhile, Morley would go off to college, move to the city, get a life—a large one. *None of this matters,* he told himself.

Big picture: none of this matters one bit.

But the small picture was too much on his mind. Being here, right now in the middle of it, alone with this bully, it mattered.

"So, Bent-dick, what'd we decide your phone was worth?" He pulled it from his jacket pocket and held it up to refresh Morley's memory.

"Fifty bucks," said Morley.

"Hmm. I seem to recall a hundred."

"It was fifty, yesterday."

"Yeah, well, you pissed me off today, so I'll take the fifty now and you can go round up another fifty."

Morley frowned as if he was giving Bishop's sugges-
tion some thought. Then he shook his head. "Actually,
a hundred isn't even enough, Bish. The new iPhone is
worth more than seven hundred dollars, unless you're on
a plan."

Bishop's eyes grew large. "Woo-hoo! Now you're
talking."

"But you see, I'm on a plan and with my plan the
phone's free."

"Oh, yeah?"

"Yeah," said Morley, slipping the gun out of his pocket
and pointing it at Bishop Fox's gut. For a fraction of a
second, the big guy's face clouded over. Then he jerked his
head back and chuckled. "Whoa, playtime."

"No," said Morley. "It's real." Morley watched Bishop's face, saw the smile fade. "Do you get it, Bish? You
brought this on."

"You're telling me that's real?"

"It's an MP25, semiautomatic."

"Yeah, but you don't got the balls to do nothing with
it."

Morley lowered the gun until the oily black snout was
pointing directly at Bishop's genitals. "I want my phone

back. Or you won't have any balls at all."

"Eat me, Bent-dick."

"And I want you to stop saying that. And I want you to leave me alone, okay? And I want you to fucking die, actually, but I don't want to have to be the person who does it. Which is *not* to say that I won't." His voice had climbed to cracking level. He took a deep breath. "I'm tired. I can't take any more."

Bish shoved the cell phone back into his pocket. Left his hand there. Stuck his other hand in his pocket, too. Then he looked back in the direction of the fence where his posse would be hanging, waiting to hear the punch line of the joke. You couldn't see them from here. No one could see what was going down, which was the way Morley wanted it. He could see the calculation on Bishop's face. He was nervous and trying not to show it. He looked back at the gun leveled at him. He was thinking about newscasts, Morley guessed. He was thinking how these kinds of lawless things really did happen and it was happening right now to him. It wasn't some Tarantino movie. There was no denying the gun was real. It wasn't big or fancy. It wasn't some badass Glock. It was a nasty little piece of metal garbage. But it wasn't a toy and it wasn't a starter pistol. It was hard to tell why but you couldn't mistake it.

Morley remembered the first time he saw a wolf out near the house. It ran across the road and was gone in a matter of seconds but you knew without knowing why that it was not a dog you had just seen. It was something feral and mythical.

"You are so going to regret this, Morley."

He's using my real name. Progress.

"This is so fucking not funny," said Bish, raising his voice. But there was apprehension mixed in with the anger. It gave Morley heart.

"You're right," he said. "There is nothing funny about it."

Suddenly Bish stepped toward him, and Morley thrust the gun forward, his arm straight but shaking—shaking like a twig in a windstorm. He grabbed his elbow with his left hand trying to steady himself. "Not one more step, Bish. I mean it."

Bish seemed to calm right down. "You stupid a-hole," he said, and took that one more step.

Which is when Morley fired.

And the gun went off.

And a ragged hole appeared in the aluminum siding of the equipment shed.

There hadn't been any bullets in the magazine, but there had been one—just the one—in the chamber. The sound was huge. The hole was huge, bleeding darkness. Bish stared, gape-mouthed, at the torn metal a foot away from him. He stumbled back. If *he* was surprised, Morley was even more surprised, but he couldn't lose this moment. He swallowed hard and wrestled his voice steady.

"My iPhone, Bish. Now! I won't miss again."

Bish turned to him, his eyes wild. He fished the iPhone out of his pocket and threw it on the grass at Morley's feet.

"Don't ever come near me again," said Morley, just barely managing to get it out. He could feel himself crumbling inside, feel chunks of himself falling in, walls caving, a seismic crack in the floor at the base of his skull. He would cry any moment. Could feel the tears welling up inside him. "Get out of here!" he yelled. And Bish took off.

"Fucking lunatic!" Bish yelled when he was out of sight.

He'd tell the boys at the fence. What they did with the

information, Morley couldn't even begin to guess. None of this had played out the way he had imagined it would. He hadn't fired at the shed wall as a warning. It was his shaking arm mixed with recoil. It was just pure dumb luck he hadn't killed him. Luck! He'd been aiming at Bishop Fox and he had missed, at six feet.

He dropped his arms to his side, the weight of the tiny gun too much to hold up another moment. He dropped his head. Let the tears come. He sobbed. His fingers came uncoiled and the gun fell to the ground. He buried his face in his hands. He sobbed, waiting for the authorities to come and take him away. They'd do it by the book. They'd want to take inventory of all the shit in his head.

Minutes passed into ages. No one came. When Morley could breathe properly again, he wiped the snot and tears off on his sleeve, picked up his phone, and put it in his pocket. But beyond that he couldn't move. He sank very slowly to his knees and felt along the cinder-block foundation until he found a gap. The soil under the shed was sandy, free of grass. He began to scrabble at the earth, clearing it away, clawed at it. It was soft enough that he had a hole a good eight inches deep in no time. With one last hurried look around, he thrust the gun into the hole and covered it up. He cleared the site. Stood, looked down. There was no sign. He rubbed his soiled hands on his pants, to wipe away the evidence. He'd scour his hands in the washroom, wash a layer of skin off them. Make himself clean. He moved away, turned back to look at the burial place. Took a deep breath. Then he stuck his hands in his pockets and headed back across the field toward the school. He didn't look in the direction of the smoker clan over at the fence, but he could feel their eyes on him. Feel the silence. No one spoke. He'd shut them up. For now, at least.

Zane Prosser stepped from behind the trees where he'd been hiding. He was disappointed in Morley. He had been so close to doing the right thing and saving everyone a lot of trouble. But he'd blown it. Still, you had to look on the bright side.

Zane's father was very careful about his firearms. They were always locked up and the hiding place of the key was a secret to Zane, though he had searched and searched. Anyway his father's collection was made up of rifles and shotguns. Nothing you could hide. So Morley might have failed, but he had done Zane a very big favor nonetheless.

He sighed a little.

It would have been good to have an ally, but he'd long ago stopped believing that would ever happen. There was no one on his side.

On his knees he crawled along the wall, his fingers probing, here and there. He'd heard Morley digging but he hadn't dared to look, so he didn't know exactly where the thing was buried. What had Morley called it: an MP25, semiautomatic? So, .25-caliber ammo. He could get his hands on that, easily enough, now that he had his hands on a gun. And it was here, somewhere, close at hand. He could almost feel it. He sat back on his haunches, closed his eyes, his hands resting lightly on his thighs. He listened with his whole bruised heart.

"Where are you?" he whispered.

Pssst!

SHOOT

Gregory Galloway

It was nearly midnight, and surprisingly, no one had been shot yet.

We had gone hunting at my uncle's deer lease in the morning, and came away empty when we shouldn't have. He has a system that practically serves up the deer on a silver platter. The only problem is, you still have to shoot them. You aim and fire, and we'd done it hundreds of times, but this time was different. Aim and fire. It happened twice that day, for entirely different reasons and with entirely different results.

My uncle had been tracking a couple of big bucks for the past few days. He plants clover and alfalfa and wild-flowers on his land to try and keep them coming back, and has some good white oak that keeps them happy in the fall. He's set up cameras in some of the trees so he can keep an eye on them on his computer. He'd seen three nice ones just before the season was ready to start and sent me some pictures. We were in the car and headed over to his property as soon as we could.

My uncle had a cabin about a half mile out back of his house, where the four of us stayed. It wasn't much, but we didn't need much. The cabin was small, with just the main room, a tiny kitchen off to one side, and a small bathroom with a sink, toilet, and shower. It wasn't meant for much but sleeping, with enough room to fit four sleeping bags on the floor, and someone else taking the couch. It had a fireplace and no trophies on the walls. "You take pride in the hunt," he told me when we first went hunting together five years ago, when I was twelve, "you don't take pride in the killing." He wasn't a serious man, but he took all of this seriously. He kept the cabin tidy and safe, with a mudroom to put boots and coats and stuff, and a gun safe, where he stored everything. He expected us to leave it the same way or better. He would come and check on us and maybe bring us some food from the house, but mostly he left us alone. He was good that way.

He had given us the first couple of days of the season; the rest he rented out. He made good money leasing out the cabin and providing access to the fields he owned and watched. He didn't hunt much anymore and never with a gun. He had taught me to shoot and how to hunt almost everything, squirrel and rabbit, quail and pheasant, and deer, but he was strictly bow now. He never said it, but you could tell that he thought using a gun was cheating. What he didn't think was cheating was setting up surveillance cameras and luring them with food. We didn't care; we just wanted to shoot something.

Tim had the car, but he didn't want to go. "I've been deer hunting," he said, as if that were an explanation. "Bring a book," Nick said. "Or watch a movie." Nick and I had done a lot of hunting together. We didn't really care what Tim was going to do; he wouldn't be in our deer stand. He'd be with Jacob. We only wanted him to drive.

"Look at these guys," I said, and showed him the pictures my uncle had sent me, drawing the phone back when Tim tried to take it from me. "Don't you want to shoot them? Who wouldn't want to shoot them? Who doesn't like to shoot stuff, anyway?" I'd used this sort of argument before, usually with success, but this time my own words would be used against me. Tim shrugged as if he didn't care, yet we knew he would drive us. "You can sit around here or sit around with us there," Nick said, almost losing the deal after we already had it. Tim doesn't like to be told what his options are. If you give him the either/or, he'll come up with another way, his own way. "It's my car," he said. "I'll drive it where I want to." In the end, he drove us to my uncle's cabin. It's where he wanted to go, after all, whether he would admit it or not.

It was late afternoon by the time we were packed up and on our way. I rode shotgun, and Nick and Jacob were in the back. There was no one on the road, a small, straight country highway, when Tim, out of nowhere, did a U-turn and started driving backward. Tim was always doing this kind of stuff, so much that we started calling it "going to Timland." We didn't mean it as a compliment, but Tim acted as if it was one. "You drive backward in Timland, I guess," Nick said. Tim didn't say anything. He looked over his left shoulder through the back window and kept accelerating. "Come on, Tim," I said. "We don't have time to mess around." He slammed on the brakes and brought the car to a stop in the road. He acted as if he was going to turn around again, but then, at the last moment, started driving in reverse again. "All right," I said. "You proved your point." Nick and Jacob didn't say anything.

Tim always had to prove a point, even if there wasn't anything to prove—or a point. It always had to be his idea, which is fine with me, but you'll see where it takes us, and just remember, it was Tim's idea.

We had unloaded the car when Tim realized he'd brought the wrong gun. He unzipped the carrying case and found a .22 instead of his deer rifle. "What are you going to shoot with that peashooter?" Nick said.

"My brother put it back in the wrong case," Tim said. Things were never his fault.

"I'll get a gun from my uncle," I said.

"No," Tim said. "Don't say anything to him about it."

"It's no big deal," I said. "Take mine. I'll borrow the gun. It doesn't matter."

Tim was adamant. "Don't. It's all right. I don't need to shoot. Don't say anything." Tim zipped the gun back into its case and took it out to the gun safe.

We were unrolling our sleeping bags when my uncle checked in on us. "Tim's got the couch," he said.

"He drove," I said. "It's only fair."

My uncle had brought us some breakfast sausage he'd made. It was worth the trip just for that. He also brought us some eggs; all we'd brought was a couple of big bottles of Coke and a loaf of bread, not even butter. My uncle put the sausage and eggs in the refrigerator and then showed us the most recent images of the deer. "They've been coming by the stands over by the oaks in the morning," he told us, "not too early, so you can sleep in a little if you want. No need to get up while it's still dark." He stood to leave and surveyed the room. He saw the shotguns propped in the corner or laid out on the floor. "Make sure those get in the safe before you go to bed," he told us, and then left us alone.

We all woke up in the dark and couldn't get back to sleep. No one said anything; we put on our boots and jackets and got our guns and ammunition out of the safe and walked out into the field. The sky was a timid gray, ready to be chased off by the sun. I didn't mind if we were early. I liked that time of morning, just before the sun comes up and the world is still asleep, even the trees seem like they're sleeping. It was only us and the sky that were awake.

We got to the first deer stand, and Nick and I took it. Tim and Jacob agreed to walk on to the next one. Tim had carried his .22 along; we didn't know why, but we didn't say anything, either. He wasn't going to hunt; he wasn't even going to pay attention. He already had his headphones on. He was going to sit there and stare into his phone and watch videos or something. I didn't care. I don't think Jacob cared, either.

Nick and I got comfortable in our stand and then went to work, watching and listening, and waiting. This is why I like hunting. You try to be nothing more than eyes and ears, unnoticed and totally aware of what's around you, the way the sunlight fills the field, the way it fills the empty spaces between the trees. You can almost smell the sunlight, subtle and sweet, as it warms the dead grass in the field. You notice things you don't usually pay attention to, the feel of the wind as it moves across, west to east, the sound of the birds, all of it, until you are unaware of yourself or even the person next to you. There's only the field and whatever enters it, light, sound, or, if you're lucky, a deer. I don't even really care about the deer. Some of the best hunting days I've had I've never seen a single deer. It's enough to be out there, completely out there, locked in to the field, with nothing else in your mind, nothing else mattering. The deer is almost a bonus, and on that day, we got a bonus, and then some.

I had hardly noticed when Nick raised his rifle to his shoulder. I hadn't even seen the deer. It didn't matter; it was his kill. We watched it make its way closer, strolling through the field as it had for days. I wondered if my uncle was at home watching all of this on camera. Nick waited, ready, waiting for one good shot. He took it and the deer fell. Nick lowered his rifle and we both watched as the deer got back up and ran off into the woods. We tried to see it through the trees, to tell which direction it had gone so we could follow it.

"I had him," Nick said, and I didn't doubt it. He was a better shot than I was, probably the best of the four of us. I nodded and kept my eyes on the woods, where I thought the deer had gone. Nick took a few pictures with his phone and then texted Tim and Jacob. We waited a good twenty minutes or so before we left the stand.

"I had him, I swear," Nick said as the four of us stood in the field. Tim and Jacob nodded and we walked across the field toward the trees.

There was no blood. There had been some in the field,

where the deer had fallen, but almost nothing after. Nick looked at the pictures he'd taken with his phone and then looked at the woods in front of us. We were in the right place; there just wasn't any sign of the deer. We weren't going to be able to track him, and Tim wanted to leave. We didn't leave; instead, the three of us continued on into the woods, and Tim followed. "Maybe he's up ahead. How far could he go?" Tim said, and put his headphones back on.

We looked for a long time. We looked at every tree and every blade of grass and every fallen leaf, looking for a sign, something that would lead us somewhere. We looked together, then we fanned out and walked through the woods in a broken line, like you see people do when they're looking for a murder victim on a cop show. We were detectives, and we liked it, or most of us did. Tim gave up after a couple of hours.

"This is officially pointless," he said. He was right, but we weren't ready to call it. "I'm going back to the cabin." We let him go, knowing we should have gone, too, but the three of us stayed and continued our search, more out of obstinance than anything.

* * *

We didn't get back to the cabin until after two. Tim was asleep on the couch and woke up when we came in. We were tired and starving. I scrambled up a dozen of the eggs on the small propane stove and cooked up a pound of the sausage. The smell of the sausage filled the cabin and my friends sat with plates and forks in their hands, waiting. We ate it all and then cooked up the other dozen eggs and ate all that.

Jacob and Tim did the dishes. "I should go back out," Nick said.

"You're not going to find him," Tim said.

"Where did you hit him?" Jacob asked, wiping the last of the plates with a towel.

"I thought I had him in the boiler room," Nick said. "Obviously I didn't."

Tim shook his head. "You're too good of a shot for that. You were aiming for the head shot."

"I took the safe shot," Nick said. "I missed, that's it."

"Head shot," Tim said. "You thought you'd brag about it. Probably hit him in the ear."

"It doesn't matter," Jacob said.

"I want him to admit it," Tim said.

"I couldn't even hit him in the gut," Nick said. "I

wasn't trying to get tricky."

"That's it then," I said.

"That's it then," Tim said. "I was only trying to help him out. We all know he's too good a shot, but if you want me to think he botched the boiler room, that's fine, but somebody please tell him to stop talking about going back out there. Not now and not later."

There was no point in going back. I was tired and settled into my sleeping bag and closed my eyes.

When I woke up, it was dark outside. Tim was talking. "So you're saying under the right conditions, you would do it." I didn't need any more context to know that he was playing his "conditional" game. Tim liked to pose hypothetical questions to get us to admit, or to prove without our admission, that we were all moral relativists, capable of doing about anything under the right circumstances. "Would you ever eat human flesh?" he might start, then lead you down a path where you would have to admit that you would. "What if you were in a plane crash in the mountains, and the only thing to eat were the dead passengers in the snow?" And that would be one of the tamer ones. He was talking to Jacob now, getting him to admit something finally. I sat up and saw Tim holding his .22 from the gun safe.

"What are you doing?" I said.

"I was trying to let him shoot me," Tim said.

"It needs to go back in the safe," I said.

"Don't you want to watch me shoot him?" Jacob said.

Jacob and Tim might think it was funny, but my uncle wouldn't like a gun being out of the safe. I held out my hand and knew I was embarrassing myself but I didn't care. Tim finally handed over the rifle and I took it out to the mudroom and put the gun back in the safe. You could see my uncle's house at night if the lights were on. They weren't on. *Maybe he'll come by later,* I thought.

Nick was up when I got back. The three of them were sitting on the couch, Tim in the middle, with Jacob and Nick on either side, peering over Tim's shoulder, looking at something on his phone.

It was an old black-and-white video, with really only eight seconds of video; the rest of it was about two minutes of narration. They were transfixed.

"Look at this," Nick said to me, and I went and stood behind the couch.

Tim started it over again and pointed to some text

below the video. "At seven forty-five p.m. I was shot in the arm by my friend." Tim skipped ahead and showed me the footage. Two men stood in a small room, one standing up against the wall as another stood about ten or fifteen feet away, aiming a rifle at the first man. Then he shot him in the arm and the shot man walks calmly toward the guy who shot him. There's two still photos after that, one of the guy's bleeding arm, then one of him being bandaged.

"It's fake," I said.

"It's not fake," Tim said. "It's a performance art thing. This guy, he's an artist, Chris Burden. He did this as an art thing, in front of an audience."

"Why didn't they stop it?" I said.

"That's one of the questions," Tim said. "Don't you think? Why didn't they stop it?"

"Because they're an audience," Jacob said. "Maybe they didn't think he would actually shoot him."

"Or maybe they knew it was fake," I said. "Like a movie."

"It's not fake," Tim said. "I've looked into it."

"He's a little obsessed with it," Jacob said.

Tim was like that. He couldn't let things go. And when he was like this, you had to either follow him or let him think he was the one leading.

"It's not fake," Tim repeated.

"So what? Now you want to shoot someone?"

"Why not?" Tim said.

"Because it's stupid." I could see that Jacob and Nick were already on board. Typical.

"No one's going to get hurt," Tim said.

"That's clearly not true."

"Well, not hurt bad. I read about it. He got shot in the arm and then had a doctor treat him. We could do this. We do it and then immediately get to the hospital. It's, like, fifteen minutes away, fifteen tops. We go in and tell them it was an accident. We have to commit to that and stick with it."

"What if they call the cops?" Nick said.

"It was an accident," Tim said. "That's all we have to say."

"How did it happen?" I said.

"We didn't know the gun was loaded. We weren't familiar with the gun, something like that."

"It already doesn't make sense," I said. "It won't make sense."

"We just need to figure out the story," Tim said. "We

need to figure it out and stick with it."

"Forget it," I said. "No one's shooting a gun in here."

"I'm willing to be the one who gets shot," Tim said.

"No," I said.

"Why?" Nick said.

"Because I'm not going to get hurt, not bad, anyway. And I'll have a great story to tell. Think about it. I can tell any girl that I got shot, and can tell her any story about how it happened, and show her the place where I got shot. I can get mileage out of this. For, like, ever."

"What girls?" Nick said.

"I don't know," Tim said. "Any girls, girls I meet in college next year. I can tell them all about it."

"Couldn't you just make it up? You could tell them the story without actually having to get shot. What would they know?"

"You're missing the point," Tim said.

"What is the point?" I asked.

"The point is to shoot so it means something for once. Anybody can shoot a deer. How many people can shoot another person?"

"Anybody can," Nick said. "It happens every day."

"Everybody does it," I said.

"Not like this," Tim said. "This is different and you know it."

"You want to get shot just to impress some girls you don't even know," Nick said.

"There are worse reasons to do something," Tim said. "Wars have been fought to impress women. Besides, it's only part of it. Don't you want to know what it's like?"

"I know what it's like," Nick said. "It's going to hurt like hell."

"You don't know," Tim said.

"I don't know what it's like to have my hand chopped off, either, but I'm not asking you to go get the ax," Nick said.

Tim was getting fed up, but not enough to drop it. "No one's asking you to get your hand chopped off, and no one's asking you to get shot. I'm not even asking you to do the shooting. You'd probably miss my arm and shoot me in the chest, where you should have shot that deer."

Nick dropped his head and stayed quiet.

"I'm the one who's willing to get shot," Tim said. "For my own reasons."

"Just because isn't good enough," I said. "Not to be shot or to be the one shooting."

"It's my story," Tim said. "And the one who does the shooting can tell people he shot a guy. How great is that? How many people can say that? 'Yeah, I shot a guy once. With a rifle.' Beats most people's lame-ass stories. Might even beat my story about getting shot."

"I'll do it," Jacob said. "I mean, why not?"

"You're not doing it," I said. "This is stupid."

"It's no more or less stupid than shooting anything else," Tim said. "We just wasted the whole day chasing after some stupid deer. What's the whole sense in any of that? In fact, this makes more sense. We're both agreeing to it, we're going to take every precaution we can, and it's not going to be a big deal."

"You don't know," I said. "Jacob could miss and hit you in the chest or neck or somewhere. You could have more damage to your arm than you think. You don't know. There's no point to it."

"It's a .22," Tim said. "You can't hurt anything with a .22."

"There's that couple in Missouri that killed all those people who came to their house, killed them all with a .22 rifle," Nick said. "The wife made a bed quilt out of scraps of their clothes, remember?"

"What are you talking about?" Tim said. "That's not happening. None of that has anything to do with this. It's going to be about the same as getting hit with a baseball."

"Get me a baseball, then," I said. "I'll throw it at you all day long."

"We're going to do this," Nick said. "You don't have to be part of it. Go up to your uncle's house, and just go with us to the hospital."

"I can't," I said.

"He can't," Nick said. "He has to be part of it."

"How do you figure?"

"The safe, that's how," Nick said. "How else would we get the .22?"

"We could say he gave us the combination," Jacob said.

"I might as well be part of it, then," I said, "for all the trouble I'd be in."

"You might as well," Nick said. "Who doesn't like to shoot stuff, anyway? Isn't that what you're always saying? You should do the shooting."

"No, I shouldn't," I said. "I don't care if you do it without me, but I'm not doing it. But you'd better figure out your story. None of it makes sense."

We talked through the story, or numerous versions

of it, over and over, trying to get it to seem plausible. I thought that the more they talked it through, the more they would see that it didn't make any sense, and they'd give up. Instead, the more they talked about it, the more it seemed like an inevitability. Jacob was going to shoot Tim, and Nick was on board or indifferent, and what I thought didn't matter. Even I was getting to the point where I didn't really care. Let Tim get shot, if that's what he wanted. If he thought he could figure it out, who was I to stand in his way?

It seemed like a certainty, but it hadn't happened yet. "This isn't going to work," Tim finally said. "Not like this." He leaned forward on the couch and gave me his full attention. "It has to be you."

I should have known that it would somehow come back to me. "It has to be you," Tim said. "You're the only one who can get away with it."

"How do you figure that?"

"Your uncle," he said. "You have to get the gun. You have to do the shooting. It doesn't work any other way. Besides, your uncle will forgive you. Not the rest of us. He'd never let us come back here. He'd never forgive us for the shooting, and especially not for opening the safe, even if you'd given us the combination. But he'd forgive you."

"Maybe not," I said, but no one else agreed. "And what about your parents? They won't forgive me."

"It was an accident," Tim said. "If we stick with that, they'll get over it."

"They won't care," I said. "All they'll think is that I shot you."

"You'll have to live with that," Tim said. I would have to live with it. "But you'd know that I let you. It was my fault."

"You're asking me to take on a bunch of trouble just to shoot you. I can shoot you anytime. Why does it have to be tonight? Let's do it back home; let's wait so we don't have to drag my uncle into it."

"It has to be tonight," Tim said. "It's perfect tonight." This is where it becomes almost impossible to talk with Tim. His ideas become cold, immovable facts and he counts on the rest of us going along.

"And what if I tell people?" I said. "What if they get so mad, my uncle, my parents, your parents, that I tell them that it was all your idea, that you wanted to be shot?"

Tim shrugged. "You won't tell them. But if you do, it doesn't really matter what I wanted. You pulled the trigger. It was both of us. That's why we stick with the story. It was an accident. We were packing our guns for the morning, and we brought all the guns into the cabin. You were teasing me about the .22 and picked it up. You didn't know it was loaded, and you were kidding around and accidentally pulled the trigger. It was an accident. That's all. How mad can they be?"

"They'll be out of their heads mad," I said.

"It'll be a scratch," Tim said. "They'll be relieved."

"Let me see the video again," I said. I didn't watch Chris Burden; I watched his friend, the one with the rifle. He stands with feet apart, his right foot in front of the left, both of them parallel to the wall behind Burden, the rifle raised to the friend's right shoulder, his left hand on the trigger. They're both in the frame, about fifteen feet apart. You can't see the friend's face as it's hidden by a big bush of hair. You don't even know his name. All Burden says is, "At seven forty-five p.m. I was shot in the left arm by a friend." He's absolutely precise about the time, but nondescript about the friend. Maybe Tim was right; in his story no one would care; they would only care that he was shot.

"We're going to film it, right?" Jacob said.

"We can't film it," Nick said. "We have to stick to the story. We can't have some video of it. Then we'll all be in trouble."

It didn't matter. We were well into Timland. "It's only for us," Tim said. "Use my camera." He handed his phone to Jacob.

It was almost midnight; we'd been talking about it for hours, talking about it until it had weight and momentum and expectations, like a movie that once started can't be abandoned, but has to be watched until the end. I was going to do it. I didn't see any other way. It was Tim's movie; it was his idea.

There is something immeasurably satisfying about shooting a gun. If you haven't done it, I can't explain it, and I'm not sure I understand it, anyway. It's mechanical and physical at the same time; it takes concentration and control and yet is nothing more than squeezing a trigger. Such a small action causing so much violence. Maybe that's it. I don't know, but I know that I have always liked it. Lots of people do.

The trick is to not think about it, not in the whole, anyway. You have to restrict your thinking, concentrate not on the person, but on the arm, not even on the arm, on the small target area. You have to disconnect the arm from the person, the target from the arm; you have to think in abstract terms, like *target*, *objective*, dehumanized words, so the thought of shooting a person, especially your friend, doesn't creep into your mind. But do you have to do that? Isn't that the test? Should you separate the act from the person, the victim from the violence inflicted upon him? Or maybe you should be aware, painfully aware. It shouldn't be an easy, callous, soulless thing, should it, to shoot another person? Even if it's planned, well planned so that no one gets seriously hurt, it still shouldn't be easy, it shouldn't be allowed, really.

I thought they would stop me.

I walked to the mudroom and took the .22 out of the safe. It was still dark in the place where my uncle's house stood. Maybe they were still gone, or maybe they'd come back and had gone to bed. You couldn't tell. I thought he would have checked in with us, but maybe not. I checked the rifle; it had a bullet in the chamber. I checked the safety and made sure it was on. It seemed as if it was going to happen, whether I wanted it to or not, but I was the one who had to pull the trigger. I reminded myself of that.

Nothing could happen without me, no matter what Tim or any of them wanted.

Tim stood against the wall of the cabin, his legs slightly apart, braced for whatever was to come, his left arm held out slightly away from his body, hanging straight down, a slender target. Jacob looked at the image of Chris Burden and made minor adjustments to the way Tim was standing. We figured that was the important thing. I could do whatever I wanted, just as long as I could hit the arm. I wasn't sure that I could.

I raised the rifle to my shoulder and looked down the barrel with my hand nowhere near the trigger. I've done my share of shooting; I haven't killed that many animals, mostly squirrels and rabbits and some birds, even shot a couple of deer. I've never thought about it, never had any hesitation or second thoughts. They have thoughts and feelings and consciousness just like we do, parents and families, and feel pain just like we do, but "You shoot them, don't you?" Tim had said. "You don't have any trouble shooting them. So why not shoot me in the arm, just nick the arm, that's all you have to do. I want to know what it feels like. Aren't you the least bit curious about it?" I wasn't curious. The less I thought about it, the better. I looked down the barrel and saw his arm, tried not to see it, but see instead the fabric of his shirt, the dark patch of cloth, nothing but a dark patch of cloth against the white paint of the wall behind him. I lowered the gun.

"I'm calmer about this than you are," Tim said.

"You want to switch places?"

"It has to be you."

"Just come look."

"Don't think about it, just shoot. Then we'll get the hell out of here. It will be all over. Just shoot."

There were only about ten people who watched Chris Burden get shot in the arm, Tim said. I wondered what that meant. Were there only ten people interested in seeing someone get shot in front of them or were there only ten people invited to watch? And were they instructed to not intervene, to not try and stop the shooting of another person, or were they disinterested or thought it was fake or that it wouldn't really happen? I didn't know if Tim really wanted to go through with it or if he was sure I wouldn't pull the trigger. He seemed to really want to know what it was like to be shot in the arm; he wanted to have that experience and that story. Maybe he trusted me to do it right. It was hard to tell with him, and the more we'd talked, the less certain I was. Jacob was standing off to the side, waiting with Tim's phone in his hand, and Nick was standing behind us somewhere, out of sight. They weren't going to say anything; they wouldn't do anything. They would be happy enough no matter what happened, I thought. But who wouldn't want to see some guy get shot? But who would?

"You don't want to go your whole life without shooting someone, do you?" Tim had said to Nick.

"Actually, I would. Why would I shoot someone?"

"Because you can," Tim said. "This is a free pass. Maybe your only chance to do it and get away with it."

"If I started shooting, I'm not sure I'd ever stop," Jacob joked, but it was probably true. It wasn't a big stretch to see Jacob as one of those quiet types who snaps one day, and the next thing you know he's boiling bones on the stove and making quilts out of his victims' clothes.

But I was the one holding the gun, aiming it at another person, doing the one thing you're told to never do, until they train you to do it in the army or police department or something. They train you not to think about it, don't they? They prove the thing that Tim always argued, that we're all relativists, that under the right conditions, we're all capable of anything. Did I want to help prove him right? I looked down the barrel and saw nothing but blue cloth. It wasn't Tim; it wasn't even his arm. It was just a spot, a target like any other, and all I had to do was pull the trigger like I'd done hundreds of times. I wouldn't miss. The bullet would hit the cloth, maybe just to the right of his actual arm, grazing him and lodging in the wall behind him. It wouldn't be an accident, but it would seem like one. Maybe we'd get away with it. Maybe no one would hate me too much, and Tim would have his scar and his story and would know what it feels like to be shot, and I'd know what it was like to shoot someone. I would give Tim everything he wanted, and I'd have to take the blame. Only in Tim's world is the guy getting shot better off than the one doing the shooting. But do you think about these things or put them out of your mind? There had been nothing but talk about it, nothing but thinking. That part was over, wasn't it? There was nothing left to do but squeeze the trigger. That's how the story has to end, isn't it? It was such a small thing to do, but no one would understand. Everything would be a lie after that. I thought Tim would stop it, that he couldn't just stand there and wait for it like that. I couldn't look at him, but he couldn't look back at me, either, could he? Could he stare at the rifle and wait for it? Jacob and Nick said nothing; they would say nothing. It was between Tim and me and I tried not to think about him. Someone should have stopped it. There was nothing to do but put an end to it, to stop it myself, one way or the other.

The door opened and my uncle said something. I don't know what it was. Maybe it wasn't even a word; maybe it was nothing more than a shocked sound. I didn't hear anything but a pop, a split-second crack that seemed slightly out of reach, maybe not even inside the cabin, as if it had happened behind my uncle, right when he spoke, something snapping in the dark outside the door. It wasn't until I lowered the gun that I realized what had happened.

We had rehearsed our lie, gone over it again and again. It was an accident. It was an accident. That's all we had to say. Only now it wasn't a lie. And no one believes me.

THE BODYGUARD: A FABLE

Ron Koertge

Donald watched his mate nibble at tall fescue. It was autumn, a beautiful time of the year. The August heat was gone and with it the flies and other pests. Winter was right around the corner but there was still plenty of food, room to roam and to gambol, really, if the mood struck.

Things were almost perfect. Except for one thing.

"Dixie, I've been thinking."

She raised her attractive head. Her large, soft ears wig-wagged. She said, "Oh, dear."

Donald frowned. "That was funny once. A long time ago."

"Sorry. What were you thinking?"

"I feel, I don't know, not like myself. Me, a

sixteen-point buck. Me, who poses majestically on his own private crag. Me, whose picture is on every yellow 'Watch for Deer' sign—hooves tucked, head high, a ten from even the German judge."

"I know what it is, dear. Excuse me. Darling. I feel it, too. It's hunting season."

Donald sighed. "I look at you grazing peacefully, and I think about tomorrow and men with guns and I hate it that I can't protect you."

"I was talking to Donna down at the salt lick the other day and she said Derek is depressed, too. Plus they're having trouble with their son Diego. He's been darting across Route 22 every time he sees a pickup with a gun rack. Teasing the driver. Daring him. Exactly what we don't need at this time of the year."

Donald shook his head. "Kids. I was that way once. Now when autumn rolls around, all I can think about is where to hide, and it just pisses me off. We were born here. This is our home. Just because humans have rifles and a piece of paper that says they can shoot us doesn't make this forest theirs. I'm tired of running, Dixie. I can hardly look at myself in a pool of still water." He pawed at the ground fiercely. "Running scared. What kind of a way to live is that?"

"There were some close calls last year. Deborah still has a scar on her flank and we know what happened to Dudley."

"Strapped to the fender of a Ford F-150. Don't remind me."

Donald looked around. An owl sat atop a tall pine. Two skunks ambled past. A dozen rabbits nibbled and ogled one another.

"Look at those dumb bunnies," Donald said. "Not a care in the world. Nothing to do but race around pointlessly, poop, and go at it like . . . well, like rabbits. No hunter ever talks about how he stalked a bunny for hours until he got a clear shot."

Donald nuzzled his mate. He put his head across her slender neck and she leaned into him.

"If anything happened to you," she said, "I don't know what I'd do."

Donald stopped mid-nuzzle. His eyes narrowed. "You know what? We should hire a bodyguard."

Dixie stepped away so she could look directly at him. "A bodyguard. When you say things like that, it makes me want to put my hoof to your forehead and check for a raging fever. You are clearly delirious."

"Just hear me out. What do you fight fire with? With fire, that's what. In this case, firepower."

Dixie looked at her handsome mate dubiously. "A human bodyguard."

"Well, yes. Our forest friends, nice as they are, are woefully lacking the requisite trigger finger."

"Not raccoons."

They paused to consider that—a raccoon. All sixteen pounds of him. Standing on his hind legs. With a pistol.

Dixie started to laugh first. "The mask," she sputtered.

"Exactly! It's too perfect."

They let the hilarity wind down before Dixie said, "Not that I agree with you, but since an armed, medium-sized mammal isn't the answer, how would we go about hiring a bodyguard?"

"I've been thinking about that. Remember when the campgrounds were fully funded and we used to wander down and give tourists a thrill?"

"I do," said Dixie. "It was all, 'There's Bambi!' I loved that."

"Then we'd bound away followed by the flash of iPhones only to circle around so we could lie in the underbrush and watch their TVs."

"That was fun. We spent our second anniversary at Silver Lake Campground."

"Exactly. And what was all the news about on Channel 13?"

"Celebrity rehab?"

"Hard news, Dixie."

"You tell me."

"Unemployment," said Donald. "And the widespread economic and social effects thereof."

Dixie leaned to nibble. She chewed thoughtfully. "I think I see where you're going with this."

"Hundreds of people out of work. Thousands." He raised one hoof and scratched himself. "But how would we pay him? It's all humans care about."

Dixie said, "I know where there's some money."

"You clever doe. Where?"

"At those cabins up past the lake, the ones the forest service used to rent. They're all deserted now. Deborah and I were up there a week or so ago. You know how bears are when it comes to cold pizza. Half the cabins had their doors torn off. And Deborah is such a snoop. But guess what she found nosing around in a cigar box right next to some disgusting playing cards—a roll of bills."

Donald looked very interested. "How much?"

"A lot. I know I saw fifties and twenties."

"That's perfect. Do you think the money is still there?"

"Why wouldn't it be?"

"Let's bound up there and see. If it is, we'll take the cash and tonight we'll make our way down to the outskirts of Stink City and scout out those double-wides. There's always some poor guy sitting out back with a cold six-pack."

"Should we tell any of the other deer?"

Donald shook his head. "Not yet. We're hiring a bodyguard, not an army."

That evening Donald and Dixie made their way toward Stink City, the derisive name all the animals used for the small town at the foot of the mountain. They waited at the two-lane blacktop until they could cross safely, then—using some silent oil rigs and the chassis of abandoned cars for cover—they headed for the nearest Waverlee trailers.

The first one sat unevenly on cinder blocks. They skirted the dark backyard and made their way around to the front where windows were either missing or were mere aluminum frames with no glass. Flimsy curtains stirred in the breeze. A piece of paper fluttered from the front door. On it, in large letters, one word: FORE-CLOSURE.

Silently they moved on. Two hundred yards away a figure sat in a low beach chair, an Igloo cooler by his side, a paperback book facedown in the dirt.

"He smells," said Dixie.

"They all smell. But he's not armed."

"He kind of looks like a bear."

"He's not a bear. He's just hairy. C'mon."

They moved closer. Even closer. The man wore cutoff jeans and a faded tank top with three words on it—I'M WITH STUPID.

Donald cleared his throat. "Excuse me," he said.

The man looked. Blinked. Looked away. Looked again. Muttered, "Holy crap!" He tried to get up. Fell back. Tried again. Failed again.

Donald began. "We were wondering—"

The man made a guttural sound; he slammed the lid of the cooler and thrust the whole thing away from him. "That's it," he muttered.

"Are you all right?" asked Dixie.

"No. Hell, no. I'm not all right. I'm delirious or something."

Donald asked, "If this isn't a good time, we could come back—"

"Hey, now. No. There's no good time to be talkin' to a wild animal out in my own backyard."

"My name is Donald. And this is my mate, Dixie."

The man took a long drink of beer. "Okay. Sure. This here is absolutely the delirious part. Not just talkin' animals, but talkin' animals with names."

"We've always talked," said Donald. "Just not to humans."

The man's eyes narrowed. "So why start now?"

"We have a proposition for you," said Donald.

"All right. Fine. I'm gonna wake up in the morning and tell my wife about the crazy dream I had, so let's just go all the way with it. What kind of proposition are we talkin' about?"

"It's actually quite simple. We want you to guard us when hunting season opens tomorrow. I'm assuming, of course, you have a rifle?"

The man nodded. "More than one. And what exactly would I be guarding you all from?"

"You, in a way. Humans. Hunters."

The deer could almost see the man's mind work. Then he exclaimed, "Oh, hell, no. I'm no murderer. What kind of leaves have you two been chewin'?"

Dixie pointed out, "But you murder us."

He shook his head violently. "That's different. That's hunting. That's sportsmanship and animal management and, okay, I admit it, lots of fun, too. What you're asking me to do is a whole other—"

Donald moved a little closer. "We don't want you to harm anybody. All we want you to do is frighten them. Drive them away so they won't come back."

The man stirred and the aluminum chair groaned and swayed. "Oh. Well. Now we're talking about security work."

"We could call it that."

His eyes narrowed again. He licked his chapped lips. "For how much?"

Dixie leaned and spat out the wad of bills she'd secreted in her cheek. Daintily, using her right hoof, she separated the fives from the tens and twenties. "Sorry about the dampness, but—"

He eyed the money greedily. "Not a problem." He

picked up a fifty-dollar bill. "For one day's work, right?"

"Let's see how it goes," Donald said. "And as for tomorrow—half now. Half after."

Dixie leaned and, with one flick of her tongue, took back some of the money.

The man tucked damp bills into his pocket. "'Let's see how it goes.' That's fair." He extended his right hand. "I'm Randy."

Donald lifted his hoof. He hesitated. So did Randy, who finally drew his hand back and said, "That's just too weird."

Donald nodded. "But we will see you in the morning. Take the old forest service road that leads to the falls. Wait by the big rock. We'll find you. Come before dawn! That's important. And don't tell anybody."

Randy smirked. "Are you kidding? Who'd believe me if I did?"

Early next morning, Donald and Dixie spotted their bodyguard making his way on foot up the dirt road. He was in full-on hunting regalia—camo everything, including his hat and boots.

"Are you alone?" asked Donald.

"What's it look like?" Randy rubbed at his beard.

"Do you have a bandanna?"

"I might. What for?"

Dixie asked, "Would you be so kind as to blindfold yourself? The forest has its secrets, and we want to keep it that way."

Even as he complied, Randy muttered, "I can't believe I'm doin' this. If I'd-a just stayed in the service—three hots and a cot, money in the bank, people salutin' me all day—"

"Ready?" asked Donald.

"Sure. Let's go if we're goin'."

The deer led Randy into the woods. Nudging him left and right, warning him about fallen trees or low-hanging branches.

"So clumsy," Dixie whispered. "He couldn't jump over a chipmunk without falling on his fat face."

"Humans," Donald mused. "Clumsy, cruel, *and* a long life span. It isn't fair."

Thirty minutes later, when they were sure Randy was disoriented, they led him into a clearing where the other animals waited—dozing, nibbling, gossiping.

But all that stopped when Dixie, Donald, and Randy burst into their midst.

"RUN!!"

Dixie darted forward. "No, no, no. It's fine. He's not going to hurt any of you. He's with us. He's our bodyguard."

Bancroft Bear looked out from behind a tree. Wolf and Fox peeked out from behind Bancroft. Raccoons and rabbits froze.

"Are you crazy?" asked Bob Cat.

"It's an experiment," said Donald. "No running for Dixie and me. No hiding. If this is successful, there are a lot of unemployed hunters in Stink City. Every one of you could have his own bodyguard! There's a lot of bad guys with guns; we'll have good guys with guns."

"Wait'll you take that blindfold off," ventured Serena Skunk. "Then we'll see how good a guy he is."

Randy spoke up. "Wait just a damn minute. I've been out of work for longer than I want to think about. I contracted to do the strangest job anybody ever heard of for X number of dollars, and that's what I'll do. I got integrity. I don't give a crap about you all. Just boogie on outta here for all I care. Then I'll get on with what I was hired to do, which is to intercept and engage the enemy, and drive him back to the extraction point."

Bancroft rumbled, "Come again?"

"Shoot at the sons of bitches till they run back to their trucks."

"What about the day after tomorrow?" asked Octavius Owl. "Won't they return? Humans don't take insults and humiliation lightly."

Randy turned in Octavius's direction. "They might," he admitted, "but they might not. Lots of places to hunt around here. Why come back someplace they was shot at?"

The animals exchanged troubled glances.

"Well, I don't know about the rest of you, but I am out of here," said Fox. "They don't call me 'wily' for nothing."

"Coyotes are wily," said Walter Wolf. "Foxes are crazy. But not crazy enough to be part of this. Thank Nature I'm a lone wolf. It takes two to hatch a nutball scheme like this."

"Let's just everybody settle down and leave Randy alone to do his job," said Donald.

The animals—all but the two deer—scattered, disappeared with barely a trace. They might have melted into the landscape. The clearing fell silent.

Donald whispered, "I hope this was a good idea."

"Too late now," replied Dixie. And then to Randy, "We'll be nearby."

He fumbled with his blindfold, blinked, looked around. Raised his weapon. "Just stay behind me!"

They followed their bodyguard from a distance. They heard the hunters before he did, and froze before he lifted his hand. They watched him lie behind a fallen log and half cover himself with leaves. They watched him wait until men appeared, walking four abreast. They listened to the sharp report of Randy's weapon, and they heard the sound of heavy bodies ducking for cover.

"Hey! What the hell? How much hunter orange do we have to wear?"

Randy pulled off another four rounds.

"Hey, man. What's your problem?"

More rounds, which elicited more scrambling, more swearing, followed by running.

"Look at them go!" said Donald. "Now they know what it feels like!"

"What a wonderful sight," said Dixie. "I never thought I'd live to see the day—"

"This isn't over, you crazy bastard," one of the men

shouted. "You don't know who you're messin' with!"

Randy waited. Dixie and Donald waited, their ears up. Finally, nothing. Not a sound. The forest always got that way after gunshots.

Randy stood up. "That's that then." He reloaded as he walked back toward the deer. Donald stepped in front of his mate.

Randy laughed as he slung the rifle over his shoulder. "Don't worry, you still owe me money. But I'll tell you what I think for free. Those boys might be back, after all, and if I'm right, me and my friends should be here." He eyed the deer greedily. "Have you all got any more cash?" Casually he let his rifle point in their direction.

Donald gave Dixie an almost imperceptible nod as he shouted, "What's that!?"

As Randy turned, the deer bounded away. If their bodyguard lifted his Remington 700, they didn't see it.

Just before dusk, Donald and Dixie met the other animals again. They hung their heads.

"Lie down with humans, get up with fleas," said Walter. "I hope you know that given the opportunity he would have shot you. *And* you put us all in jeopardy."

"I said it was an experiment," replied Donald without conviction.

"An experiment in fraternizing with the enemy," muttered Serena.

Donald snapped, "We were thinking survival. Nobody wants your little black-and-white head on his wall."

"Hey, just because I'm small, you think my life is worth less than yours? Thanks a lot, you size-ist ninny."

Vincent Vole stepped forward. "Paraphrasing the great Josiah Wedgewood, 'Am I not an animal and a brother?' And to paraphrase the even greater William Shakespeare, 'If you shoot me, do I not bleed?'"

Dixie looked at her mate. "Vincent's right. We didn't think things through."

Serena asked, "How could you stand to get within a hundred yards of that so-called bodyguard? Sweat, tobacco, beer, and what is that concoction they splash on themselves?"

"Aftershave," said Vincent.

"How do they ever manage to mate? Does the female hold her nose?"

The animals paused and pictured that. Soon the titters began and those grew into howls and roars. Octavius Owl spit up a pellet he laughed so hard.

When things settled down, Donald vowed, "Believe me. It'll never happen again."

Vincent spoke up. "Perhaps this experience will serve as a reminder of our natural superiority. We kill to live, never for amusement, malice, or sport. We respect one another. We allow for differences."

Dixie looked thoughtful. "Randy might say he kills to live, also. To put, if you'll pardon the expression, meat on the table."

"How can you defend him?" asked Bancroft. "He'd shoot you in a heartbeat."

"If I would stand still long enough, which I wouldn't. I haven't lived five whole years by being careless. And, anyway, I was brought up to see both sides of any situation."

Octavius observed, "Well, you're about to see my backside because I am going north for a while."

Many of the animals nodded. Bancroft ambled for a dozen yards, then turned and looked back.

"You go on," said Dixie. "We have some business to take care of."

Donald looked surprised. "What business is that?"

"Just follow me."

* * *

It was just past dusk when the two deer made their way toward Stink City again. Past the forlorn oil pumps again. Past the rusted chassis again. And into Randy's backyard.

There he was in shorts and flip-flops despite the cool weather. Donald cleared his throat. Randy put down his paperback mystery.

"Well, look who's here," he said. "I never thought I'd see you two again."

Donald moved a step closer. "You did a hundred percent of what we agreed you'd do for fifty percent of your salary. Remember—half before, half after? There was a little misunderstanding right after. We thought you might . . . When you pointed that gun . . . That's why we bolted. But we're here now and we want to settle up."

Daintily, Dixie spat out a damp cud of cash. She pawed at it with her hoof.

Randy smiled and got to his feet. "This'll really come in handy. I'm obliged to you."

They looked at one another across a great divide that had been narrowed now to just a few feet. Donald started to say something, then didn't. Randy began to count the money, then stopped.

They heard the sound of a car door slamming. Some-one yelled, "Randy! Where the hell are you, man?"

"Those'll be some friends of mine," Randy said. "Prob-ably best you all get on out of here before—"

But they were already gone, headed for the forest that seemed, anyway, to go on forever.

FIGHT OR FLIGHT

Alex Flinn

May 2012

"Top ten weapons?" the dude to my right says VERY
LOUDLY to be heard through his ear protection and over
the other shooters. "I can get it down to three."

"Three?" Mr. Angelo pauses and even puts down his
.22. "Which three?"

"Easy," the guy says. "First, a good shotgun—twelve
gauge, model eight-seventy. Second, a rifle, not too big,
but not too small, either. And third, a good, reliable .22
like this one here." He pats his gun. "That'd be enough
for a survival situation."

"Basic survival, yeah." Mr. Angelo nods. "I agree with you there. But what about if the shit really hits the fan—the Barackalypse?"

My older sister, Kate, on my other side, nudges me and mouths, "Barackalypse?" She doesn't even try to stifle her grin. I roll my eyes and line up my shot.

"Obamageddon?" the guy says. "That's easy—a good semiautomatic. But that's not gonna happen."

"Your lips to God's ears," Mr. Angelo says, lifting his gun again. I lift mine as well and angle my body forty-five degrees from the target, which is a picture of a zombie.

"So, Mel," Kate yells. "Did you hear about that face-eater guy?"

"What face-eater guy?" I'm used to this. Kate has never been into shooting. She's a vegetarian and says shooting animals is gross. But considering we're shooting sheets of paper, I don't see what that has to do with anything. She finds it amusing when Mr. Angelo talks about Obama's reelection possibly resulting in the End of Days. I find it sort of scary—mostly because I know he's serious. Like, what if he lost it and went on a shooting rampage the day after the election?

"It happened yesterday," she continues. "The cops

shot this guy on the MacArthur Causeway—he was eating another guy's face."

"And by 'eating another guy's face,' you mean . . . ?"

"I mean it literally. Face-eating."

"Sure." *Gross.* I aim at the zombie's forehead and squeeze the trigger. A perfect shot. Of course, is the brain the right place to hit a zombie when they have no brains? I fire five more at various vital organs for good measure, hoping maybe Kate will forget about this gross line of conversation. I check my gun bag for more ammo, but I'm out. I wait until Dad finishes shooting, then approach him, avoiding Kate's eyes. I do not want to hear about face-eaters.

Dad shakes his head, indicating he's out, too. When we went to Walmart last week, they had no .22 ammo. In fact, they were sold out of a lot of ammo, but they did have the shirt he's wearing, the one that says, GUNS DON'T KILL PEOPLE. FATHERS WITH PRETTY DAUGHTERS KILL PEOPLE. He promised only to wear it here. I begged him not to buy it, but he thinks it's funny.

It's so not. But in my family, everyone but me has a bizarre sense of humor that gets set off by stuff like face-eating jokes.

Case in point:

"Why did the zombie go to the dentist?" he says to Kate. Without waiting for her reply, he says, "To improve his bite."

Kate groans, and I say, "That's really not funny. A guy was eating another guy's face."

He shrugs. "Maybe if they had global health care, they'd take care of the mentally ill, and that kind of thing wouldn't happen."

At the moment Dad starts his pro-Obamacare rant, I expect the shooting around us to suddenly stop and everyone around us to stare. It's something my dad usually doesn't mention at the range: He's a Democrat. A liberal. He voted for Obama.

Bang!

But it doesn't stop, and I hold up my hand to get him to quit it, because I don't want to get into an argument with all these guys with guns.

I go to the bench and pack up my stuff, then wait until the range is cold and collect my zombie target. It looks thoroughly undead-dead. I smile.

Kate follows me out. "So do you think it was a sign of the zombie apocalypse?"

I know she's back on the face-eater topic. "Meth-head, more likely."

"Who's a meth-head?" Mr. Angelo has followed us out. With my eyes, I plead with Kate not to tell him. It's better not to engage him on current events.

But Kate says, "The face-eater guy."

Mr. Angelo shakes his head, knowing exactly what she's talking about. "Lot of sickos out there. That's why it's important to be prepared, not get caught with your hands in your pockets when the liberals let everything go south."

I look away. "Be Prepared" is Mr. Angelo's motto, but that doesn't make him a Boy Scout.

Things I like about shooting:

- **Being better at it than my dad (and, needless to say, Kate).** Well, sometimes. When I was little, and he used to take me shooting, we had these cool splatter targets that turned different fluorescent colors with every bullet that hit, and I'd save them until my mom got tired of stepping on them and threw them away.

- **Bonding with my dad.** He went shooting with his dad when he was a kid, and even though we don't have a whole lot in common, this is something we like to do.

- **Power.** You can have this little tiny gun, even a pink-and-purple sparkly one like I had when I was a kid, and it can actually kill someone. I mean, don't get me wrong, I'm not going to kill someone. I mean, yeah, if they were coming at me in the middle of the night, and I had my gun with me, I would, but that's unlikely because our guns are in a gun safe in my dad's closet. My dad's lectured me over and over again about respecting guns and how to handle them. So I'd never actually aim one at someone, but I could. And, even though that's scary, it's sort of awesome. I'm five feet tall (same height as Annie Oakley, the great sharpshooter), cute, and look powerless. But I'm not.

Things I don't like about shooting:

- **Two words: Mr. Angelo.** Mr. Angelo is my PE teacher from elementary school, and he's one of those guys that make gun owners look crazy. If he was a character on television, I'd think he was too stereotypical, but here he is, in my real life, actually existing.

Right now, he's wearing enough camo to guest on *Duck Dynasty*—pants, jacket, hat, sneakers, even his T-shirt says PREPPER in matching green camo. A prepper (sadly, I know this) is a kind of survivalist who's getting ready for the End of Days. When I had Mr. Angelo for PE, he always wore a polo and Bermuda shorts. I guess he still does—to school—but we get to see the real him at the range.

"Lunch?" Mr. Angelo asks Dad. "The usual place?"

"I have a lot of homework," I say at the same time Dad says, "Great idea."

Dad looks at me. "It's just lunch. You gotta eat some-time."

"There's nothing for Kate to eat there."

"I don't mind just having French fries," Kate says.

"Of course you don't," I say, because I know she's just doing it to bug me.

"And they have the best corn," she adds.

We head to our car. We didn't come with Mr. Angelo. He just seems to show up at the gun range every time we're here lately. Maybe he's following us or maybe he just goes every day.

Mr. Angelo was my favorite teacher in elementary

school. I was scared of the ball when we played softball, and everyone made fun of me, but he was really encouraging and kept giving me extra turns, catching pop-ups until I got it.

I miss that guy.

The good thing about The Pit barbecue, where we go to eat, is that it's out in the middle of the Everglades, so no one I know goes there. If that wasn't true, I'd definitely have gotten a case of raging diarrhea instead of agreeing to go with Dad in his embarrassing T-shirt, and Mr. Angelo in his embarrassing . . . well, everything. The food here is good, the closest to Southern barbecue you can find in Miami, and it's not so far out that I can't get an internet connection on my phone (there is none at the gun range), the better to tune out the conversation.

"So you're having trouble finding ammo?" Angelo's saying to Dad. "I can help you out there."

"You know someplace that still has it?" Dad's interested.

"Someplace real close to home. I make it myself, in my garage."

Of course you do.

"You make your own ammo?" Kate kicks me under the table. "Isn't that fascinating, Mel?"

Don't involve me in this.

"Hmm," I say, because it's the least I can say.

"How'd you get into that?" Kate asks a bit too perkily.

"Necessity." Angelo raps his knuckles against the table. "Have to be prepared for when Obama's goons come in their black helicopters to take our guns away."

Goons. The thought of our elegant president having anything approaching goons almost makes me laugh. Almost. But I've heard it enough times to know not to engage him.

And so does Kate. And yet she does. Engage him, I mean.

"Do you really think that's going to happen?" She rolls her corn in butter. "It hasn't happened yet, and Obama's been in office over three years."

Angelo starts to answer, but Kate keeps going. "There are people out there who say the whole paranoia about Obama taking guns away is just propaganda from the gun industry to make more sales."

By *people*, she means Dad. Dad says that all the time. He also says gun sales have actually almost doubled under

Obama, with more permits issued than in the previous Republican administration.

Angelo laughs and starts to wind up for what I'm sure is going to be a big speech when it happens:

Brendan Hoyt and the entire Palmetto High Environmental Club walk in.

Oh, jeez.

I know why they're here. There was a nature walk in the Everglades this morning and, of course, it ended right now.

There's some kind of unwritten rule that, if you love the environment, you have to hate guns. I have no idea why—some kind of Democrat handbook I didn't receive. I'm the only idiot out there who loves both. So I turn my face to the wall and pretend not to be there as Angelo makes a speech that begins with an explanation that Obama's awaiting reelection before he shows his true colors and ends with him waving his arms around and shouting, "In the words of that great American Charlton Heston, they'll take away my gun when they pry it from my cold, dead hands!"

And then, he sits and takes an audible chomp on his pulled-pork sandwich.

I sneak a look away from the wall.

And see the entire Environmental Club staring at us.

"Melanie?" that's Brendan. He's in the environmental club *and* the Young Democrats *and* he's my secret crush. He has blond hair and these long eyelashes that perfectly frame his gray eyes. In fact, if I'd known he was going on the nature walk thing, I'd definitely have gone myself.

"Heyyyyy." I picture how we must look, Mr. Angelo with fresh-killed meat dripping from his lips.

Don't be stupid. Everyone eats pulled pork at The Pit.

And Dad in his crazy-embarrassing T-shirt.

Sure enough, Brendan turns his gray eyes on Dad, and so does everyone else, looking from Dad to Mr. Angelo, Mr. Angelo to Dad, as if they're watching tennis on TV.

I wrack my brain for a logical explanation as to who these people are and why I'm with them, one that doesn't involve me actually being related to them.

"I thought you were going on the nature walk," Brendan says. "You said you were when we talked yesterday."

And it dawns on me. Brendan wasn't going to go, but he went because I said I was. And I was going to go, but I skipped because he wasn't going.

Star-crossed lovers, like Romeo and Juliet. Or something.

"That is so fascinating," Kate's saying to Mr. Angelo.

Shut up, Kate. Shut up, Kate.

"Are you doing the thing where you put away extra food and supplies in case of the apocalypse?" she asks.

"Barackalypse," Mr. Angelo corrects her, and I see Brendan's eyebrows rise.

"And yes," Mr. Angelo continues, "we've stored up some extra food. Of course, we do that for hurricane season, anyway. But Terri's canning, too."

I've come up with my story: Angelo is a relative (a distant one) from out of town, and we had to take him out. Everyone has crazy relatives. They'll understand.

But, suddenly, Ashley Garcia steps out of the group and says, "Mr. Angelo? You were my PE teacher in elementary school."

And, at that same moment, Dad stands, stretches out his hand to Brendan, and says, "Hello. I'm Melanie's father. We've been out shooting today."

I die. Just die.

Except I don't die. Dying would be easy. I just sit there, living the whole thing in slow motion, like a scene in a movie, that old one my dad likes, where the woman's trying to pull a baby carriage down a huge staircase, and you know the mob hit men are about to show up.

Just like that.

Dad's standing there, hand out, wearing his FATHERS WITH PRETTY DAUGHTERS KILL PEOPLE shirt.

Mr. Angelo's standing there, talking about laying up supplies for the biblical End of Days, and obviously, he's not from out of town.

Ashley's standing there, really, really close to Brendan.

Everyone I know now thinks I'm a weirdo.

In science, we learned about something called a "fight-or-flight response." When an animal (or a human) is confronted with danger, he reacts with an instinct either to fight or to flee. There are those who say "Stand Your Ground" laws, which protect gun owners who shoot intruders on their property, make people more likely to fight.

But I do what any normal fifteen-year-old girl would do.

I flee.

I grab Dad's keys off the table, say I feel sick, and run to the car.

* * *

I keep up the sick act for the rest of the weekend and Monday, too. My mother tends to believe us about being sick when we say we're sick on Saturday. After all, why would we miss our day off? But, of course, Kate tells her I'm being a brat and skipping.

So, Monday night, Mom demands to see actual symptoms.

I want to just tell her the truth, that I lied to get out of going to school because her husband completely humiliated me in front of everyone I know. That, in fact, I need to transfer schools. But to do that would make her question me (harder) every time I'm sick for the rest of my life. I'd never be able to stay home for cramps or get picked up from school for a headache.

Finally I decide it's not worth it. I should suck it up and go to school.

I was soooo wrong.

I talk Mom into driving me (still a little sick) so I can skip the bus and, also, get there at the very last second to avoid conversation.

But still, when I sit by Ashley first period, she giggles and says, "Hey, Melanie, you packing heat?"

It's like that in every class, with someone making funny remarks or pretending they're shooting an Uzi. I try to text Mom to pick me up, but she says no.

When I see Brendan, I avoid eye contact. He says, "I heard you were sick."

He's being nice, but I still can't look at him. He thinks I'm a weirdo, that my family are weirdos. Maybe we are.

That night at dinner, I tell my dad, "I'm not going shooting anymore if Mr. Angelo's going to be there."

Dad shrugs. "I don't invite him. I can't make him not go. The gun range is a public place."

"Then I guess I'm not going. Why does he have to be such a nutcase?"

My father purses his lips. "It takes all kinds. I hope you'll change your mind. I like having something we can do together."

I used to.

"So they think that guy was on bath salts," Kate says.

"What guy?" my mother asks, and I give her a look. How can she not know what guy? It's literally all Kate talks about lately, other than school.

"The stupid face-eater guy," I say.

"His name was Rudy Eugene," Kate corrects. "He was on bath salts."

"Bath salts?" my mom asks. "Like Calgon?"

Kate rolls her eyes. "It's a kind of synthetic drug."

"How do you know this?" Mom puts down her fork. "How do you know about synthetic drugs?"

"They say he may just have gotten some bad marijuana," Dad says. "Don't do drugs. They turn you into a zombie."

I cringe. He's such a goof.

"I still think he was an actual zombie," Kate says.

"Well, it's good they shot him before he spread the zombie virus," Dad jokes.

"Can I be excused?" I say. "I've lost my appetite."

That night, Mr. Angelo comes over with a box of homemade ammo and some mangoes his wife canned. Dad wants me to come out and say hi, be polite. I pretend to be asleep.

The days pass. Kate informs us that a guy in Maryland was arrested for eating his roommate's heart and brains. Then weeks go by. The *Herald* reports that only marijuana was found in Rudy Eugene's system. Kate says that proves he was a real zombie. Dad says it just proves drugs are bad.

I volunteer for the Obama campaign at school, and people sort of forget that I'm supposed to be a Second Amendment nut. Sort of.

One day, we're sitting in a Young Democrats meeting, talking about how to get out the vote. Brendan actually saved a seat for me, which is huge. Ashley walked in ahead of me, and I heard her ask if the seat was taken. Then he said it was saved and called me over.

Yeah.

"Anyone have any other suggestions?" Jorge Casas, the president of the club, asks.

Ashley raises her hand. "We could reach out to other groups we're involved with. Like maybe Melanie could contact the NRA."

Everyone stares at me. The National Rifle Association. Cute.

"What are you talking about?" Brendan asks.

"Don't act stupid," Ashley says. "We all know Melanie's a gun nut."

"I heard she was a Second Amendment freak," someone else says.

Everyone laughs, and I want to leave. To fly. But I

can't. Not with everyone staring at me, already thinking that me and my family are complete idiots. I can't fly.

So I fight.

"Yeah, that's it, Ashley. I'm a Second Amendment freak. I'm not in the NRA, but I am a card-carrying member of two different gun ranges. So what? I like to shoot paper targets—ooh, scary. And what if I am a Second Amendment freak, anyway? Isn't the Second Amendment part of the Constitution—as valid as the First or the Fifth or the Fourteenth? Doesn't it protect our right to bear arms? Aren't Young Democrats *for* the Constitution?" I stop to breathe and look at everyone. They're silent.

I continue. "Not everyone who likes to shoot or even hunt is a crazy who wants to own Uzis or doesn't believe in background checks. Not everyone thinks the framers of the Constitution were talking about machine guns. There are plenty of responsible gun owners like my dad—like me—who shoot targets as a sport, because it releases tension, tension caused by dealing with idiots."

I look at Ashley, to let her know exactly who I mean.

"I don't happen to believe that all my ideas need to come from the same place," I finish.

And then, I fly. Or, at least, I stomp off in a hurry, leaving everyone gaping.

That night, Brendan texts me, asking if I want to hang out at the mall Saturday.

I say yes.

School ends. Brendan and I become sort of a thing. "I like a woman who speaks her mind," he says. Kate reads *World War Z* and *The Zombie Survival Guide* and researches signs of the zombie apocalypse. (According to her, there are none.) The Associated Press reports on a Canadian porn actor who dismembered his victim and mailed body parts to people. In late June, the Center for Disease Control issues a statement that there are no zombies. A spokesman says, "The CDC does not know of a virus or condition that would reanimate the dead." It's in the Huffington Post.

I still don't go shooting with Dad. Instead, Brendan and I start going biking on Saturdays. We plan a big ride at Shark Valley, to make up for the nature walk I missed, but it's summer and the mosquitoes are bad, so for now, we just ride to the park and the little beach near my house.

We're on our way back from the beach Saturday, riding through my neighborhood. I love riding. It's so peaceful. Brendan's ahead of me, which I like because I can admire his legs. Still, it seems eerily quiet as we ride past Coral Reef Park. Then, I hear sirens in the distance. I wonder what that is.

Probably nothing. I move my gaze up to Brendan's butt.

He says something I don't hear.

"What?" Reluctantly I stand up on my bike and pedal hard to catch up with him.

"I said that's weird!" he yells. "There's no one in the park. Usually on a Saturday, there'd be tons of people, kids playing baseball and stuff."

It's true. There's no one there. No one on the fields, not even on the playground.

Then, I see it, a strange, hulking shape on the ground. It looks like an animal, crouched over its prey.

As we get closer, I see it's human.

Or maybe not human anymore.

Oh. My. God.

It's a man—a zombie—eating another man.

It lifts its head, sniffing the air.

"Come on!" I scream at Brendan.

He sees it, too. We both begin to pedal, faster, harder, looking away from what we can't, don't, want to see. But there are more, more, a child crouched over a woman, a woman eating a man, and as we pedal away, one begins to pursue us. I don't look back.

Brendan yells at me, but his words get lost in the sound of thundering footsteps and the whirring of pedals against road.

Then I hear him.

"Do you have any guns at your house?"

"Damn right I do!"

We pedal hard, hard enough that the tromping footsteps behind us fade to a dim echo. Yet, I know it's not over.

We've lost the zombie by the time we reach my house. Still, we abandon our bikes on the driveway, not wanting to take the time to put them in the garage. We may need them again, for speed. But first, we need power.

Power.

I find my keys and open the door with trembling fingers. No one's home. Where are they? No time. I lock the door.

"Come on!" I tell Brendan. I run to my parents' bedroom, find the gun safe, open it.

My .22 is there, unused.

I look in Dad's drawer and find what I'm looking for, Mr. Angelo's homemade ammo.

I load the magazine.

I hear Brendan breathing beside me. He's never been close to a gun before, but what we just saw was scarier. I turn and look at him. He's totally freaked out, mouth open, eyes wide.

He doesn't speak for a moment, but when he does, he says, "So . . . you're gonna . . . shoot . . . ah . . . zombies with that?"

I've been all adrenaline up until now. Up until now, it hasn't hit me. There are zombies. In Miami. At the park. Eating people. Like Kate's crazy, obsessive thing isn't actually crazy.

Where is Kate, anyway?

To Brendan, I say, "I'd rather not. I'm low on bullets, and we don't know how many are out there."

And I don't want to go outside and see my neighbors getting eaten.

"Good point," Brendan says. "We'll hide in here.

Maybe we should put on the news."

We do. It's on every station. Zombie apocalypse. This is not a drill.

Where is Kate? And Dad? And Mom?

I call Dad. It goes straight to voice mail. I bet he's at the range, in the middle of the Glades with no reception. My mom is visiting my grandmother in the assisted living facility, far west of us.

Hopefully they're safe.

Brendan's parents answer. They're at his house, safe, but they think he should stay inside.

I try Kate. No answer.

Oh, shit. Why no answer? I try again. Kate is big on not answering the phone. I text her.

The news reporter is in a helicopter, the camera panning empty beaches and streets filled with charging zombies.

And then, I hear a squeal of brakes in the driveway.

I fly to the front window. It's Kate's Prius. There's something on the hood.

A man.

A zombie. She hit him with the car.

But it's moving. It's standing, and as it does, I see Kate,

running for the door.

I dash to meet her, opening it just as she reaches it.

The zombie's right behind her, bigger than my zombie target and so much scarier. It still looks human, except for the wild look in its eyes. There's no blood. It hasn't fed yet.

I raise the gun I'm still holding, and I shoot.

In the head, then the heart.

It pitches forward.

I shoot two more bullets into it.

Power.

Then I slam the door.

I throw my arms around Kate. We're trembling.

I'm in the bedroom, reloading, when I get a text from Dad. Meet him and Mom at the Angelos.

Mr. Angelo may have been wrong about the reason. He may be wrong about a lot of things. But he was right about being prepared.

I go to the living room where Kate and Brendan are watching the carnage on TV.

"Come on," I tell them.

"Where?" Brendan asks. Behind him, on our big TV, there's a helicopter view of hundreds of zombies swarming over the Seven Mile Bridge from Key West. They look like they're coming straight for us.

"I know someone who can help us," I say. "Friend of the family."

I take my gun, and we run for the car.

CERTIFIED DEACTIVATED

Chris Lynch

It was somehow more humiliating when she tried to make me feel better. Pristine, my girlfriend, who should've been my wife by then. She was behind me, leaning into me tight, while I gripped the top rail of the lower deck of the ass end of the ferry, slurping back to Lundy Lee from the Big Island. My hands were on the underside of the rail, shoulder height, like I was a weight lifter halfway through a clean and jerk that would raise the boat right up off the water. Her hands were on the topside of that same rail, like she was pushing me back down. I'm not tall. But I am clean. You do what you can. Clean jerk.

"Stop saying that," she said just as we hit that moment when the ship's engines powered way down, signaling the invisible line crossed between the wild of open water and the hard rules and boundaries of harbor. "You are not a jerk, you are a romantic."

"Same thing," I said.

"Stop it now, I mean it," Pristine said, but how much could she mean it? She was laughing and squeezing me harder as if I was a little kid needing restraining. "It was our day out, baby, and nobody else's. God was just pissed off because we weren't doing it in a church and so he wasn't invited. He ruins everything, especially weddings, which is why you never find him at anything even remotely fun."

I had never been to a wedding, so this and a lot more was news to me.

Usually I loved this ferry. It was one of the true special things about Lundy Lee and the place I came to whenever I had time and nice weather and an unclear head. The *Lucky Buoy*, it's called, and I hopped on and traveled out to the Big Island and back whenever . . . you know, just whenever. And every time, I returned somehow and somewhat better for it. Met Pristine on one of those very trips, the one time when I came back not only somehow better, but *way how* better. We were gonna be

married, me and Pristine, so in my book the *Lucky Buoy*
could sink tomorrow and still be the luckiest buoy I ever
grabbed on to.

"Well, there was no wedding, anyway, was there, Pristine? So we can't even blame *him* for ruining it."

"There wasn't, no. But who cares? Just the fact that
you believed it was even possible, and that you could pull
the whole thing off without consulting not one single
other person on planet Earth makes the day more special
for me than any ol' wedding ever could be."

"I consulted *you*, though, Pristine, and that's all that
really matters after all."

"Except that no, actually, you didn't."

"Except I did. Remember, we talked about it that time
after I warned you that a corn dog was not seafaring food
and you got one, anyway, and were throwing up over the
side? I told you then, he's a *captain,* for shit's sake. Did I
make that up? Captains of boats have the power to marry
people when they are out at sea, everybody knows that.
Everybody has always known that, even the stupidest people know it. It's tradition, and it's custom, and it's famous.
One of those famous things that everybody is supposed
to understand. It's *historical*, is what it is, and everybody

should understand *historical*, and one of the main things that drew me to a place like Lundy Lee in the first place was that this was one of those places, *those* places, where *historical* isn't dead at all. It matters. It works. And this should have worked just the way it was *supposed* to even if I had overlooked advance planning and licenses and all that crap that isn't even romantic at all. Boat, plus captain, is supposed to equal married, that's all I know."

Pristine was not talking now, even though I had left the space open for that. Still squeezing, however, and probably harder than I had ever been squeezed before.

"You, ya daffy duck, are the only thing I have ever met that works the way it's *supposed* to. And *nothing* I know of is supposed to work the way you do. Not in real life."

See, and that was it. Why this lady here deserved everything and more than I could ever give her, but still I had to give it everything I'd got. And this, *this* was not good enough.

It was humiliating. Pristine rated so much better than this. And eventually she would find what she deserved, and she would get what she deserved.

The moments when I accidentally remembered that it probably would not include me, those were bad moments.

My eyes squibbled laser-fast side to side. I had to close them tight and grab on to something or I'd fall flat on my nose. It sounds funny, but it was really sore when it happened.

"That's why it's not gonna *be* real life, honey," I said. "Not for us. Not ever. It's gonna be so much better than real life."

It had to be. It seriously had to be.

And it could be. It was possible. A lot of things folks said were just "dream droolings," even I knew that. But this was not that, mostly because of the money. I was practically wealthy, because of the job I got at the spit-shiny new-built factory eight miles outside Lundy Lee. I worked there for pretty much the premier natural-edible-collagen-sausage-casing company in the world. They had a great reputation if you knew the gristle-and-guts side of the business of making smelly, disgusting beasts into quality savory main dishes and snack foods. Which, I happened to know, because of the time I spent mostly hosing blood off the walls of Carlton's small abattoir back home. It was the only job I ever had before this one, and Carlton only let me work because he owed my mom some serious favor. Because, she said, he killed my father with Dad's own vintage Colt Hammer thirty-two-inch twelve gauge and she testified that it was an accident. They were all friends. The Colt Hammer was so beautiful, all blue and sleek, and I used to sneak to the gun closet at night just to stroke on it. I wasn't allowed in the daytime. Licked it from time to time and I always expected it to taste and feel like a blueberry Popsicle though it never did. I wasn't disappointed just the same.

I never had any idea how much truth was in the details of all that, but there were at least three large-caliber firearms I had seen in Carlton's office. And with all the blood and flesh and chopping up of carcasses going on, there never seemed quite the right time to bring it up. And we never talked. But there was no uncertainty in the fact that even though Carlton employed me, it was not because he wanted to.

Then he found out, through industry connections, that there was a job at a plant at a location far away. How would I like to earn three times the salary, he asked, making the premier natural edible sausage casings in the world? Because wouldn't you just know there was some guy out there who owed *him* a big favor. I couldn't even imagine what horrible thing that guy had done, but I wound up working second shift with a pay differential that provided a standard of living that I gathered was above average for the region around my new adopted home.

So now I had the standard. Living was going to have to be up to me.

"Because whoever came to a place like Lundy Lee looking for real life, anyway? Nobody, is who," said the Reverend St. Paul, loudly answering his own loud question. He waved us over to his table where he sat eating a hoisin chicken ciabatta that was without question built from ice-cream scoops of the same fatty play-dough fraud of a sandwich I was splitting with Pristine.

I had seen him a few times on the ferry, just as I had seen a number of other folks regularly making use of the reasonably priced, highly salted air and food and fantasy offered by the *Lucky Buoy*. He was a waver, a friendly, smiley waver-on-the-waves, the kind that people tell you to watch out for. But he never seemed diddle-prone or on the prowl to me in any of his greetings, and I oughtta have known.

Because while I have never been regular handsome, I have always been small, and my arms and legs move like they're rusted inside, from the stupid arthritis and the congenital-heart-defect shit God brought me for my first birthday. Jesus, imagine what he would have brought for a wedding present. And so with all that, mostly I've always been on my own. Mostly isolated, mostly drifting, except for the three months I was imprisoned at Carlton's for eight hours a day. Unwatched by anybody you'd love to have watching you. Mesmerizing to the other ones, the bullies, creeps, and freaks.

Watchers love the Unwatched the way cheetahs love three-legged antelope, that I have learned. And the Unwatched get the sense eventually, and can feel the heat from a fair distance away.

One would expect this guy to be one of *them*, opportunist types. But he didn't watch like that. He watched me like he watched the cook chopping green peppers and red onions, and like he watched the unmanned lighthouse, and the minke whale that breached one time and definitely laughed at everybody on board the *Lucky Buoy* before disappearing again.

And even if the Reverend St. Paul was one of them he

wouldn't be doing that kind of watching now, perving on the sad-sexy gimp, because I had a lady on my stiff little arm, and now he could see. Everyone would see, one by one by one, and it wouldn't even get old. I was not alone now and I was never gonna be alone again, either.

We were on the return ferry, back from the Big Island and the stupid wedding that wasn't, on this steely, squally Saturday late afternoon when there were only very few and very surly passengers making the trip. The sky and the sea and the cafeteria ladies were all just about the exact same gray lumpy mass. And sorry, but I felt the need to point out to this lady that my food had been falsely advertised. The "pulled pork" in the sandwich she had just shuffleboarded across the counter at me had no way been *pulled* at anytime between when the poor pig was yanked backward out of his mother's unthinkable behind and when he was extracted from the wrong end of an industrial meat-rending machine. I know from experience there is no right end of such a machine. Okay, so I was at fault there in terms of strict logic, but management should have conceded my point and my refund immediately. It had to be the king shit of wedding days, it really did.

Instead, the lady had to point out the absurdity of

someone as obviously all wrong as me demanding proper barbecue, in a place like this, on a day like this. And that if I was really thinking about whatever the "real world" might be (I probably needed to stop referring like some expert to a world I had never even seen photos of), I should probably disembark at Lundy Lee, start walking south, and continue walking, forever.

That was when the reverend invited us to sit with him.

"Aw, don't be a grouch," he said as I took a seat and stared back in the direction of the service counter. "That was pretty funny."

"No, it wasn't," Pristine said, defending me the way I dreamed she always would, now and forever, amen.

"This is Pristine," I said. "She loves me and we're almost married."

"Well, almost congratulations then," he said, reaching across the table and shaking her hand.

She slightly turned on him. "What about you? Are you *funny*, too? Mister whatever your name is?"

"I am not funny," he said. "Not in the way you are implying. And my name is Reverend St. Paul. But I'm not big on formality, so you can just call me Saul."

Pristine turned then, all shark teeth and smiley yet

scary like I had never seen in all the weeks we'd known each other. "Gussie, you gotta be smarter than this. That's not his name. Reverend Saul St. Paul? Who has a name like that? If a person's name sounds like a fake, then the person is probably a fake and who knows whatever real he's hiding? What else don't you know that everybody else knows?"

It was as if the spirit of the boat that I always came to for sea breeze and peace was deciding to jerk me every which way today. Then it got all mocking, I guess because I had the nerve to think I had the same rights to get happy and married and maybe even unvirginated like every damn body else. I felt like the *Lucky Buoy*, the first friend I made here, was now joining the same old bunch who took what was precious to me and waved it above my head where I couldn't reach.

"There's no need to talk to him like that," he said in my defense. If I didn't know better I'd think they were fighting over me. I wished I didn't know better.

"And there's no need for *you* to talk to him like *anything* anymore, Saint Reverend, Saul Paul, because now he's married to me."

"We're not married, though," I said sheepishly. A

sheep on a boat. That was me, perfectly me. "Remember, I got that all screwed up and the captain doesn't do that business?"

"Ah, that doesn't even matter," Pristine said, swatting her hand in the direction of Captain No-Can-Do, now navigating us into port.

"I'll marry you," the Reverend St. Paul said, kinda saintly.

"Why would I want to marry you?" Pristine said. "I only said yes to this guy after he asked me twenty-five times."

"In only three days," I said proudly.

Pristine shook her head in her way, that way, that violent whiplashing with the squint and the wince that said everything's all crazy anyhow so what the fuck to whatever. That was the look that first changed my everything, for the better and for forever.

"I meant," Reverend St. Paul said patiently, "I could perform the service."

"So, what, you have your own boat?"

"Ah, no, I have a church. A small church, small congregation, but still it's—"

"What?" She looked at me quizzically. "Why didn't

you start with this guy in the first place then?"

She already knew more about the man than I did.

"Because it never even occurred to me he might be a real minister. That's the way people seem to be around Lundy Lee. Making stuff up as they go along, which is mostly all right with me. But I thought he called himself 'reverend' the way another guy might call himself 'colonel' or 'the governor' or 'ace.' You're not expected to go around *believing* people all over the place, are you? I'd look like a dope. Anyway getting married on the water was my dream. I grew up so far away from the water, and now here we are, right on top of it. Remember, Pristine, I told you all about my dream and the water and you and everything? Remember?"

She was doing it again, the look, as if she honestly had to work any harder to make me crazy love her more than I already did.

"Just kinda came up with that *'colonel-governor-ace,'* choose-your-own-adventure idea all on your own, didja?" she said, brushing past the Reverend St. Paul and laying a big crushing hug on the very non-reverend Gus Glendower.

"I did," I said as triumphantly as I could with the air

all crushed out of my lungs.

"Gussie," she said, "you are so damn delicious you don't even know it. How did you ever make it all the way to eighteen years of age with that stuff playing around in your head while you're supposed to be making important everyday decisions like crossing streets and swallowing and shit like that?"

"I don't know, baby, but I'm pretty sure my luck was running out on that kind of danger stuff. Then you flew in like a magic I-don't-know-what at just the time to save me from myself. Now I have you to look after me. And all I ever needed was you, even before I knew there was a you, anyway. So I have everything I ever needed, don't I? Who else you know can say that, huh?"

"Nobody, sweetie," she said, squeezing my face like she was trying to shape it into a regular symmetrical face with proper nostril sizes and nerve function and all that. "Nobody, nobody, nobody."

I was standing by, just happy because it was gonna work out, as we bumped into the dock. Reverend St. Paul and Pristine were talking over finer points of how weddings are supposed to work, but I was only half listening, playing with the rings in my pocket because they were back in the game now and I could swear they were actually heating up in there. I was not realizing my dream of a wedding at sea, but I was this close to the even finer dream. When I next stepped onto the *Lucky Buoy* as the guy who was married to the prettiest passenger they ever carried.

" . . . Of course not, Reverend. For God's sake, I didn't even know I was getting married when I got on the boat. I should probably be asking you the same thing. Do *you* have a license to marry?"

Oh, jeez, Charlie Waters Junior. I totally forgot.

There he was, right there on the dock, waving and grinning and hooting and kind of dressed up for something fancy. I wave back.

How it was supposed to go was, Pristine and me would go out and get all married up romantic style, trip out to the Big Island and then right back again. Then, Charlie and whoever else of the guys I invited from work could bring their collagen-cased asses down and we'd make the whole trip again, only a party this time, a reception. But in all the what-all, I forgot.

" . . . Well, yes and no," Reverend St. Paul was saying.

"Well, so what, it's not that kind of wedding, anyway.

It's between me and Gussie and our hearts and that makes it real," Pristine was saying.

"Hey-hey, Charlie!" I called, coming down the ramp to meet him before he could come up it to meet me.

"What's going on?" he asked, shaking my hand while I looked all around to see who else had come.

"Change of venue," I said, scanning the crowd of people gathering to either greet the arrival or join the departure. I didn't recognize anybody. Bunch of sausages.

"Hey," Charlie said, and snapped his fingers in front of my face.

"Sorry," I said, looking him straight on. I noticed then he wasn't alone. "You brought a date? Did I say you could bring a date along?"

Folks were brushing past us on their way into—or more likely through—Lundy Lee. The clouds were starting to clear and the air was getting nice and fresh and the numbers lining up for the next trip out to the Big Island were way more than the ones coming back. That was supposed to be my party boat.

"What?" Charlie Waters Junior said, practically laughing in my face. I hated that on a regular day, never mind my, *my* big day. "First, Gus, it's a freakin' *ferry*. Nobody needs your permission to ride it as long as they got the fare. Second, Warren isn't a date, he's my friend."

"Hi," Warren said, leaning in and shaking my hand. "And congratulations. You must be really happy."

I shook his hand, and it was like having somebody shake you up out of a sleep or something.

What was I getting mad about? Why was I being stupid? What a nice guy this Warren guy was, shaking my hand here on my big day. He even had the gift-wrapped package under his other arm.

"Thank you, Warren. I am, actually. Really, really happy." I felt Pristine bump right up against me from behind as the last of the arrivals showed. "And *this* is why," I said, spinning around to present my bride to my guests in the proudest damn moment of my life.

Pride, funny enough, was the thing that almost kept me from ever meeting Charlie Waters Junior in the first place. He was the proprietor of his own thriving business despite being barely out of school himself, because his father died and before that his mother ran away and so there he was behind the counter of Bread and Waters Loans all by himself.

He must have seen me through the front window over and over again as I passed by about five hundred times while I scrambled over every inch of Lundy Lee when I was looking for wedding rings to get married to Pristine. Stupid me, I didn't figure that a place like the Lee wouldn't be exactly bursting with jewelry shops or wherever else rings might come from. I went to work on the bus that ran between my building and the factory and I came back on that same bus. I found places where I could get food that didn't smell so strong I couldn't take it back to my room without my landlady coming and chucking it all out into the alley again. And I found the pier that got me on the *Lucky Buoy*, and boy, that was all I thought I would need.

But then I found Pristine on the *Buoy* and I found I had other needs. Like rings. So I had to get to know the town better, and it was plain stupid prejudice that allowed me to keep walking past Charlie's place without taking so much as a peekaboo past the grating and through the glass into the reality of what actually transpired inside Bread and Waters Loans.

It was worse than stupid because it was stupid with pride. That was the thing, with my mom, that she told me constantly. That as bad as any sin is in its own right, there wasn't a single one that wasn't made worse when you swirled pride into the mix. Should've said in its own *wrong*, was what I thought now. Since they were sins, in their own wrong. Rather than right. That would be more correct and funnier. Ha. Never thought of that when my mom was saying it, only now. She never saw the humor in being funny, anyhow.

She was right, though. I was stupid with pride, not going into Bread and Waters Loans just because I was a man of means with a respectable job and money in his pocket and no need for a loan from such a place as this, some scrubby old pawnshop. Must've been where the pride came from because I never had it before. Money, I mean. Though pride I mean, as well, come to think of it 'cause I never had that, either.

But pride led to desperation, just like my mom said it would, and I could not find a wedding ring in the whole of Lundy Lee and so I stepped through the door of Charlie Waters Junior's establishment to finally see what the place was offering.

It was offering *stuff*. The place was crammed with all manner of stuff you could ever imagine.

"Can I help you, my man?" Charlie Waters Junior said when I walked toward him while spinning around to see all the stuff, ugly paintings of misshapen dogs and horses, old heavy brown suits and pale gowns in cellophane bags, creepy antique dolls with mange and chunks missing from their porcelain skulls.

"Yes, I'm getting married," I said, finally bumping right into the counter.

"Really?" he said. I had encountered fake surprise before, and this wasn't it.

"Yes," I said firmly, and with the right kind of pride that my mother could either approve of or just suck on it. "And I'm looking for some rings. Do you have any rings? Any *nice* rings?"

He had been leaning on his elbows on the counter, making him just a bit above eye level for me. He straightened up stiffly and stared down. Way down.

"Of course I do," Charlie Waters Junior said. "Loads of rings and all of them nice. This is the first place folks think about when they have a nice ring and a liquidity problem. But before I go to the nice rings drawer, you should know that we accept cash, and, ah, more cash."

It was that special swirl of pride and stupidity that

made me carry over three months' salary, including second-shift overtime pay, stuffed into my pockets. But whatever it was, I felt nothing wrong at all when I pulled bunches of the stuff out in both hands and showed it to Charlie Waters Junior's bulging eyes.

"Well," he said, "I guess I'm gonna pull out the *real* nice rings drawer."

That nice, nothing-wrong feeling didn't subside at all as he turned to the big wall of dark wood drawers behind him and I eased my money back into my warm pockets. He cursed and growled some as the drawer stuck and tried not to open. They fought it out long enough for my eyes and attention to wander up and over to a different item altogether from what I came for.

"You sell guns?" I said, knowing full well he did because I couldn't take my eyes off them.

"I know this place," Pristine said as we turned the last big sweeping bend of the shore road that had been growing grottier with every step. I found this statement a little alarming.

I had never been anywhere near this particular outer limit of the Lee front, and it made the rest of the town look something like affluent. Abandoned, rotting shacks and boardinghouses stood all along the road except for where they had fallen down completely. There were no people immediately visible, adding a lot to the apocalypsey sensation. This stretch even had its own smell, like if fish could sweat, this would be the result.

If the dark underbelly of the world had its own seaside resort, this was the place.

"You don't know this place," I said, hoping or forcing it to be the case.

"Sure, there it is, the Salvation Army Citadel, right there. They were very good to me one time when I really needed it."

It was the only stone structure on the front, and looked like a headstone for everything else.

"Well, now it's the Star of the Sea Church," Reverend St. Paul said as he led our little wedding procession up the wildly uneven flagstone path to the entrance. Pristine followed the reverend, then myself, Charlie Waters Junior, and Warren.

"SOS," I joked. "That seems about right."

Pristine whipped around to lay an angry *shush* on me. An angry, smoky *shush*.

"Baby, you know I don't like it when you smoke," I said. "Take it from somebody with a funky heart. You don't ever want to feel like I've had to feel."

She growled at me but dropped the smoke onto the flat stone.

"Hey," Charlie piped up, "is the walk made all wavy like this to make old sailors feel more welcome?"

"Old drunken sailors," Warren added.

"Well," Reverend St. Paul said as he turned the big iron key in the cranky, clanky lock, "I hope so, because old drunken sailors are very much welcome here."

It was cold inside, colder than outside, and the only light was coming through the small but numerous windows set up at various odd heights and angles of the main meeting hall. The hall itself was about the size of a primary school classroom, with two blocks of dark wooden benches divided by a middle aisle. There was a strong odor of salted wood mold that I actually found comforting, and that nearly succeeded in defeating all the other odors.

"I like it," I found myself saying.

"I love it," said the bride, taking my hand.

"Spooks the shit outta me," said Charlie Waters

Junior. "But yeah. Yeah."

We all let it hang there, some silence and scent, as we got used to where we were and what we were there for. In no order, other than me sliding right up next to Pristine, the guys all fitted into different pews and just sat.

"So," Warren said out of the stillness, "you actually try to make it, like, inviting here, to all those cracks-of-society types. Like, 'Come on, all ye sinners, bring us some game. Show me what you got'?"

"Exactly," Reverend St. Paul said. "Goddamn, I'd call it the Holy Tabernacle of Alcohol, Tobacco, and Fire-arms, put it on the roof in neon-tube lighting if it would help bring in the people who need to come in."

"Ha," Charlie said. "Rev used 'goddamn' the same way the rest of us do."

"Well done," Warren scolded him. "Think maybe this is why you don't get a lot of wedding invitations?"

There was another ebb in the flow among the wedding party until this time Pristine pushed through.

"It *was* you, wasn't it, Reverend? Taking care of me. The Salvation Army time. I do remember you. Don't I?"

I almost didn't care now what the answer was because the question was so warm, so sweet and close and grateful that I felt the fine-gauge wire *yank* more tightly around my heart than ever.

"There were a great many dedicated Soldiers who worked here over the years, and certainly you were cared for by a number of them. I may have been one."

"Can you even do weddings here?" I asked impatiently. "Is it even a church anymore? Where's the rest of the *Army*, then?"

"They do good work," Reverend St. Paul said. "But maybe a little too militaristic in their ways. I was given official marching orders to go to a new congregation. I resisted, gave up my Soldiership. Didn't matter, they were pulling out, anyway. I decided to stay. There was still important work, God's work, which needed to be done here, regardless of whatever shingle we hung over the door."

"Wow," Charlie said. "Balls, Rev. In a good way, balls, as in you've got 'em. I could never commit to a thing like that, with people like that."

"You *do*," Warren said, making both Charlie and the Reverend laugh out loud, the sounds shocking as they bounced around the stone walls and back to us.

"You are a very good man, Reverend," Pristine said

in a voice that was different from any other voice I had heard from her.

"We really need to get married now," I said, lest anybody lose sight of our mission.

"Don't do that again," Charlie Waters Junior ordered. "I mean it. Any more facial contact with the guns and they go right back up on the shelf. No lips, no noses, no cheeks, and especially no tongues on the merchandise, I don't care how much dough you got in your pockets."

"Sorry, sorry, I can't help it. They just have so much—"

"I don't care how much of it they have. It's weird. You'll ruin the finish on them, and possibly my lunch, too."

I could help myself, but it would be difficult. And I didn't want to. The thing about fine firearms is, it's always there, always. The pull, the hold, the grip it would get on me. I had always felt it intensely, like the thing itself was talking straight at me. Just looking at a proper well-made rifle, shotgun, pistol would always give me a quake-like action, from the ground and rising on up, until it was in my head, and my head was volcanic with it. It was very much like I would hear the God nuts on all the God-nut stations go on about their amazing encounters with this thing that nobody could even see but them. This was like that but not, not least because you can goddamn well see a powerful firearm when it's in the room and know you didn't just make it up.

And that was even when I could merely see it. Everyone who gets the chance to *handle* a beautifully crafted weapon does not need to be told what to feel because it is irresistible. There is power in there, of course, in the heft, the balance of the thing, the way it lies in your palm and reassures you that it is ready and so able. You can feel that *it knows*, and will do for you. That it is capable, practically without you.

But not without you.

The perfection of the sights as you line them up, the careful intricate tooling of the handle design, the exact pressure of the trigger pushing back against your pulling finger, pushing back *exactly* the right amount to teach you, only and precisely what it requires of you. The gun, in your hand, is alive. It has importance and confidence and, of course, power; of course, power, but it is so much more intricate than that. If it doesn't change you, to hold a gleaming Rossi .357 polished steel revolver, then you are beyond hope. It has to change you.

"Thought you came in for wedding rings," Charlie Waters Junior said with a dirty chuckle after some chunk of time had fallen away.

"I did," I said. "But now there's this, and this must have been part of the plan all along, because it's too exact. Too ideal."

He was back in his relaxed pose again, elbows on the counter, eyes at my level.

"So, you want the guns instead of getting married, fine. You're not the first, just in case you were wondering that."

"No, I was not wondering that, and no, not instead. As part of. The final piece. Get it? These guns are us, they are the final pieces, that make me and Pristine absolutely one together. They are *supposed* to be ours."

He stared, expressionless. "Pristine? That's really her name?"

I stared back, eye to eye, man to man, calmly letting one finger gently trace the outline of the bigger gun, drawing me a clear mental picture of it while I was looking at Charlie's eyes.

"Yeah. That is her name. Really."

His eyes creased up in a grin, and we were doing business.

"They are a stunning pair," he said, politely but definitively taking back the gun that I had not bought yet and returning it to its nesting place. The matched pair of Rossi .357s—one with a four-inch barrel and the other with a six-inch—nestled into a handsome red-silk-lined display box. They were posed as if firing at each other, which, of course, they would never be doing. Just the thought of it, and me and Pristine, made the scene look almost obscenely cute to me now. "They come with the official deactivation certificates, so you'll have no problems there. . . ."

"Come again?"

He straightened up, a little surprised. "You didn't think you were purchasing *operational* weapons here, did you?" He let his voice get louder now than at any time yet. "Because I don't have the proper license to sell anything like that." Then he dropped it so low as to be almost miming. "But we can always talk. About anything. Talking's not against the law. About anything."

He had given me enough time to realize my mistake and to also realize I didn't mind.

"Of course I knew that," I said. "But firing a fantastic piece of work like this . . . it's practically beside the point.

The power is already in there, in the gun itself and all that's gone into it, and all that it carries to you when you carry it. C'mon, you feel that, don't you? Feel it, go on, you'll understand. The real power is all right in there, even if the barrel has been filled solid with lead."

Charlie Waters Junior sighed, but gave it a try even if it was only to make a sale. He picked up both handguns, balanced each in one hand, swung them around, felt triggers and squinted over sights that he aimed at my willing forehead. He nodded happy, affectionate appreciation as he smiled through the exercise and was still smiling as he laid the lovely couple respectfully back in their presentation box.

"They could not be more beautiful if you put lipstick and big feather earrings on them. But I don't feel that thing you're talking about, sorry. The power is in the bullet. That is, in the potential to propel one through somebody's chest."

For an instant, this made me so angry. As if he had been the worst kind of rude to my personal loved ones. I even reached for the presentation box to grab it away and sweep out of the place with my guns and my great indignation. Until we both remembered they were not currently my guns.

Charlie pulled the box away, grinning slyly at me in that old familiar you-can't-reach expression I would never have to see again once I *owned this stunning matched set of polished steel Rossi .357 handguns and then had the unbelievable Pristine for my wife with Christmas cards we would send out of the two of us posed in front of a nice tree while she held up the shiny four-inch Rossi and I held up the shiny six-inch Rossi for all the world to sit up and see. We would send out thousands of those cards, and only have to send them just once.*

"I'm sorry that you can't feel it," I said. "Because it's really special, but hey, we're all different, right?"

"Oh, we are," he laughed. "Just sit behind this counter for a day, and you'll get to see how different we all really are. But it's good, all good. Good for me, good for business, good for fighting off boredom and all the other stuff."

"At least you appreciate how gorgeous they are," I said, flailing for the common ground.

"I do indeed. Babes, the two of them."

There, we rested, lounged on that common ground awkwardly. Smiling nice.

"Are we negotiating here?" he finally said, the box under his arm and ready to be packed away again on that high, special, faraway shelf that was getting higher and farther away from me as we spoke.

"No," I said.

The look of total surprise on his face was satisfying since Charlie Waters Junior had to be one of the world's premier seen-it-alls for his age division. But that satisfaction was blown clean away when he made a move in the direction of the ancient rolling librarian ladder that was going to get him to that high and faraway shelf with my guns. And I made my countermove.

"Whoa," he said as I started shoveling thickets of wadded-up cash money bills right there on the counter. He returned with the box, and it was my turn to take a step back. He picked up fistfuls of currency, looked over at me quizzically. "Okay, and so . . . ?"

"I think you'll be fair," I said, without saying that I already felt it, the thing, the power, of course, and all the rest that poor Charlie could not feel. "I trust you, which, all things considered might be crazy. . . ."

"Tell you the truth, it might be," he said without looking up from his counting.

"Well, anyway, there are a lot of *shoulds* happening together lately, like I should have met my Pristine on the *Lucky Buoy* and I should have found my way to the perfect pair of Rossi .357s to seal the deal on the ideal and unbreakable union of our wedding. And now I feel like you were a real part of all that 'cause I should have found Bread and Waters and should have found you, and with things working like they are I should let 'em roll. So you should settle on a fair price, and then just give me back whatever change I have coming to me."

Now, he stopped counting. Now, he looked up.

"This is unusual practice," he said.

I offered him empty and upturned hands. "I understand. But with the practice I've had, I don't think I'd know 'usual' if it bit me."

"Fair enough," Charlie said, and went back to figuring. He nudged the box with the guns across the counter in my direction and I ran to snatch them up so fast I banged my ribs on the counter's edge.

"You all right?" he said, straightening up and handing a neat, thin stack of bills my way.

I pocketed them without counting, then groaned a little at the pain that stuck me when I inhaled. "I'm great,"

I said, offering him my hand to shake while I pressed the box against my sore side.

"Aw, Jesus," Charley Waters Junior said before he would accept my hand. He pulled out another thin stack of bills and handed them to me to pocket, uncounted, before finally we shook.

"And I'm throwing in a pair of rings for free," he said. "Here, just root around in the drawer for a bit and I'm sure you'll be able to come up with two that look more or less alike. What's her size?"

I was just starting to rummage, after having frankly forgotten all about the rings.

"Rings have sizes?" I asked, and rummaged.

He sighed loudly. "Get her a seven. Women are mostly all sevens. Or if it's an eight, eight is fine; unless she's really big or really small these should be in the zone. Is she?"

"She's perfect."

"Of course she is. Seven'll be just right. Or eight. Right around there. She can always exchange here anytime, so no worries about that. What about yourself, like a four or something?"

"I have no idea."

He grabbed my hand, examined it up close.

"The men's and women's wedding bands are practically the same, anyway. Just keep digging, you'll be fine."

It took about ten minutes to get us somewhere around fine, but I was leaving the shop with what felt to me like an immeasurable haul of treasure, and taking it out into a fine future I never could have imagined before Lundy Lee.

Charlie Waters Junior had come out from behind the counter, wishing me all the luck in the world and holding the door for me to walk out into it.

I stopped on the threshold.

"You wanna come?" I asked.

"Come where?"

"To my wedding. Not totally planned out yet, but almost."

"You're inviting me? To your wedding?"

My heart began to hurt as the old defective stuff inside started coming back to me and making me small and stupid. Even the grand package, the presentation box with the miracle guns inside that changed things so profoundly, went suddenly powerless. Went worse than powerless, even, as the box grew larger, then heavier right there in my arms until it was gonna dwarf me and

I wouldn't be able to hold up.

"I would *love* to come to your wedding, man. That's damn decent of you."

"Oh," I said, cooling down but mostly because of the sweat misting my whole face. "Oh, excellent. I'll come by with the details when they're finalized."

"Cool."

"Cool."

"Be cool now, just be cool," the Reverend Saul St. Paul was saying to me, soothing in just the way I imagined he had soothed countless nutjobs in this same place.

"I am cool," I said, "very cool. I just asked a question. I just wanted to know if this was gonna be for real and unbreakable now, now that we are married. Really married, yeah?"

"Gus," he said, "I am an ordained minister and I have a license to marry people . . . and there are many different forms of union. In the eyes of—"

"What does that matter, baby?" Pristine asked, stepping between the minister and me. "We are together, and our special day was magic. Charlie and Warren witnessed it, and Reverend Saul said a beautiful ceremony just for us, and I'm feeling honored that he would even do that. . . ."

True. All true. It was lovely and beautiful and all true right down to the part about being honored. She was honored now by everything the reverend did. Which was great, which was fine. All I wanted was one simple answer to one simple question and he wouldn't honor me with that, would he? Yes, he was a hero and a saver of souls and tall and everything, but would we have to get all excited every time one of them came along? Because for all I knew there would be hundreds and thousands of them, and I for one was not looking forward to a life of getting honored and excited by each and every one of them that came along.

Just like that though, it was everybody. Charlie Waters Junior was up close at my shoulder and his friend Warren, who turned out to be every bit as nice a guy as he seemed, was up close at my other one. We were like a huddle, all of us. In a near-empty church or former church or halfway house or whatever this was, we needed to be in a bride-groom-minister-witness-witness huddle that frankly felt a little close.

"Pristine," Charlie said, "you just bring that ring to the shop any day you want, and we'll get you one that fits, okay?"

"Thank you, Charlie," she said, beaming at him. Really, just like they say, a beaming bride, lighting the place right up. I could see it, the light bouncing off Charlie's big mug when I turned back to see him looking at her. Then I turned to the rev to see if it was beaming off his papery old face, and there it was, bouncing right off it. He even rose up on his toes, like he needed to be that much taller than me though he was taller than me even when he sat down. That was where I met him originally, sitting there on a pew in the *Lucky Buoy*'s small tidy chapel that smelled like burnt toast. Like when somebody burns the toast and tries to cover it up with two inches of butter, exactly that smell. Met Pristine in that very same chapel, different day, same scent. Burnt-toast butter-cover smell. Still, it was the most comfortable place to be out of the weather on the *Lucky Buoy*.

"I really loved your story about your name, Reverend," Warren said. "I thought it was lovely and generous of you to include it in the ceremony. Hope it was okay to laugh."

"Of course," the reverend answered. "If you didn't laugh, that meant I bombed."

But everybody laughed, he didn't bomb, and now they laughed again. I knew the story already. It was an okay story. About his mother, and how she felt disadvantaged at naming her own child because the father's last name was such a statement already. And so how she decided to name him Saul, as a counterbalance to St. Paul, 'cause of the whole Bible story, and it's kind of funny if you look it up. And he loved her for it, and for being funny her whole life and telling the story a lot. And sure, it was a pretty good story. It was. He was lucky to have her.

I had never known a woman could be like that. I had never until recently met a woman who joked or seemed to want anybody else to joke. When I got that horrid old hurting, I knew. I knew I was in love with the woman who had given that name to Saul St. Paul. 'Cause that's what it feels like. That's just what it feels like, loving.

And now I was feeling it double, as the piercing, constricting stuff wound around my heart at the thought that I met a woman who was all that, was kind and was funny and so precisely qualified for me. I met her and I loved her and I married her.

"I have a present for you, baby," I said, tall and strong and the groom of this gathering.

"You don't have to do anything like that, Gussie," Pristine said as Warren got the package the guys had been guarding for me all day.

"Yes, I do," I said as Pristine knelt on the floor to lay the present out in front of her. All the men took steps back to make it more of a moment, to make a ring around her and her moment, which would be the moment we became unbreakable together.

It was nicely wrapped and tied, and so took her a while to get through to the prize at the center, but it was worth every bit of it for the excitement it built.

Then, down there on the floor, on her haunches, she stared into the presentation box of the two sparkling Rossi .357 revolvers, hers and his, four-inch barrel and the big six.

Time ticked slowly, loudly, as she stared into the box and finally looked up to the smile that was deep and loving but starting to hurt my cheek muscles.

"I'm sorry, baby," was all she said.

I looked all around, expecting to see my own shock on all other faces. I saw other things, which I could not even identify.

"Sorry what?" I said with some urgency.

"Sorry, but no. I don't like guns," she said in full deep throat like I never heard. *"At all."*

"Pristine," Charlie cut in, sounding as concerned as I felt, "it's okay, they don't fire anything. They are certified, they are deactivated—"

"They are *guns*," the bride said with the power to make all the saints and demons scurry to the corners.

"Right!" I cheered, the stupidest part of my brain taking over while thinking we were somehow all on the same side.

"Take them *away*, Gussie. I don't ever want to see them again. Around me, around you—"

"Did something happen, baby?" I said, approaching her slowly. "It's okay, whatever happened to you in the past, that's the past, and we can deal with anything as long as—"

"Nowwwww!" she bellowed, squeezing her hands into fists and her eyes into slits.

Maybe I was curious about what somebody else might say if I left them the space right there to say it, but curious was all it was because it was not uncertainty. And when nobody spoke, I did.

"Whatever it was," I said, calm, not unlike the good reverend's "talk 'em down" approach, "we are gonna get through this together, Pristine." Without giving it much thought, I bent down and retrieved the gun. Mine, with the six-inch barrel. Instantly it pulled all my attention. I could not stop admiring it. My heart hurt and thrilled at the same time as it caught every tiny flicker of light and brought it to its beautiful self.

"Gus," she said. "Gussie?"

"Pick yours up, Pristine," I said. "Everything will change then. If you just pick the gun up, hold it, give it a chance. I am so sure it will change everything."

"It won't," she said.

"It will."

"Get them out of here, now."

"You need to slow down, baby. Don't spoil things. I only want to share with you the most precious—"

"Choose."

"What?" This was the first time I was aware of looking away from my Rossi revolver since I picked it up. Pristine's unearthly radiant skin was picking up every bit of the facets of light the polished steel of the gun was. It was almost too much, the beauty confronting me like this was the inverted version of the whole rest of my life before. But to make me choose? Making me choose? Why should beauty bother to make you choose? Beauty has everything; why should beauty care? I always imagined beauty had no reason to care.

"I said choose, Gussie," she said, still sitting on the floor where she had opened and ruined the finest present between two people of all time. Tears I never saw before started leaking out of her, carving lines down her amazing face. It was like watching March ice cracking over the surface of a perfect pond. "It is very simple. You cannot have me and guns."

My heart was constricting, the wire digging, coiling.

"Pick it up, baby," I said. "You'll see. You'll feel it. And we'll be unbreakable together."

Her head just dropped, her shoulders shaking as she stared into her lap where her sadness of hands tried to wring the life out of each other like two nests of snakes at war.

"Okay now, Gus," the reverend said in *that* psycho-soother tone, like I was one of *them*. He put a hand on my arm and I slapped it away.

"You could have the bigger one even," I said, "with the six-inch barrel. If that's a better thing. We can try."

She just wept harder, which constricted my heart tighter, and she would not look up when I begged her to look up.

"You can't hold on to her with something like this, Gussie," the reverend said. "If that's what you're thinking."

"I know where I can get a working one," I said, still looking desperately for Pristine's face to come up to me again.

It did not. Reverend Saul St. Paul, who must have made his funny mother proud, took his hand off my arm and went to the lady, the bride, on his citadel-sanctuary floor. He said soft somethings that were undoubtedly the right somethings, and she cried a little bit less. Then he picked up the presentation box with half the present in it, and he brought it to me. As he handed it over, I felt the witnesses at my elbow.

"You're kicking me out?" I asked. "So much for Alcohol, Tobacco, and Firearms in neon then, Reverend?"

"Come on," said Charlie Waters Junior, tugging at just the right pressure on my right elbow. "We'll take that last ferry out to the Big Island and back, anyway, like the original plan. We'll have a fine time. And you'll still have the guns."

"It'll be cool," said Warren from my other elbow. Warren, who really was a good, good guy, after all.

I turned just before the exit. "Come with me on the boat, baby. Like we planned. The *Lucky Buoy,* just like we started. And like we planned. Please, Pristine? Please, like we planned?"

She was *leaning* into the reverend, who was giving her comfort now, like they do.

"I'm staying, Gussie. I'm staying here."

I became massively, blisteringly aware of the gleaming polished steel Rossi .357 revolver still in my hand as we pushed out of the church and into the world and the six-inch barrel caught every bit of light everywhere in the universe.

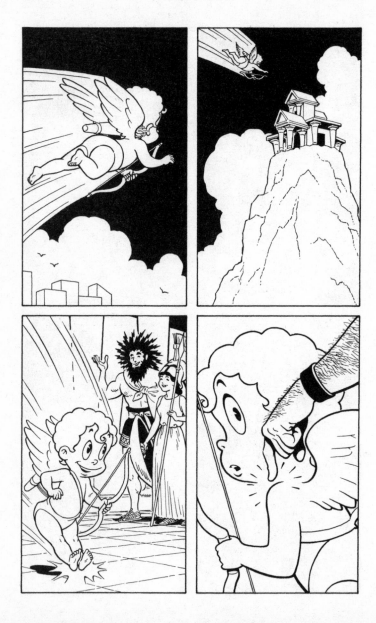

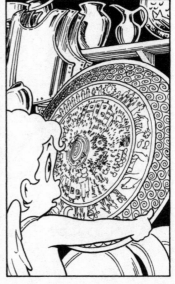

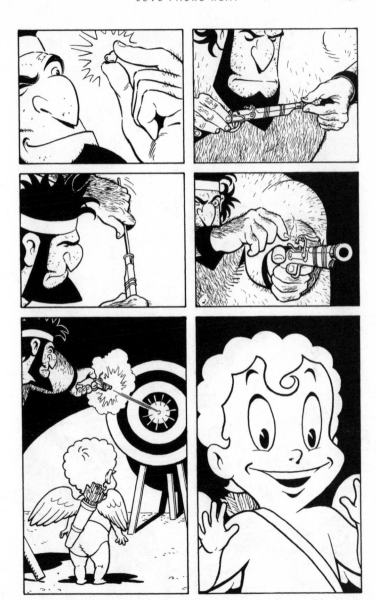

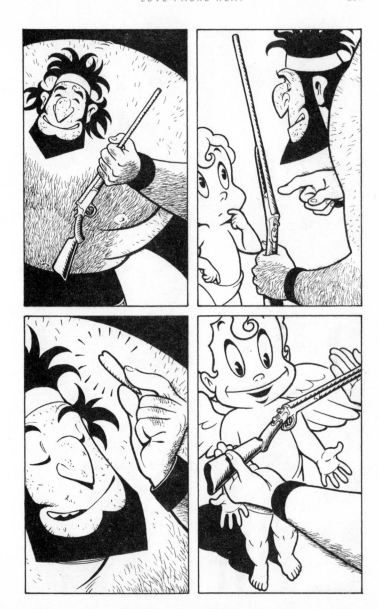

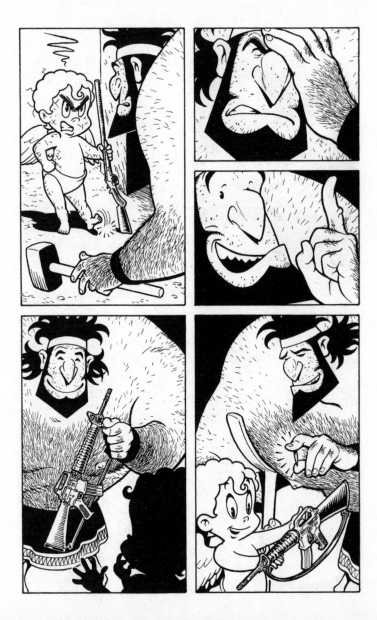

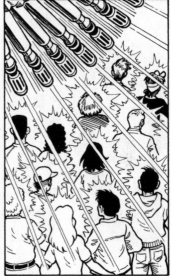

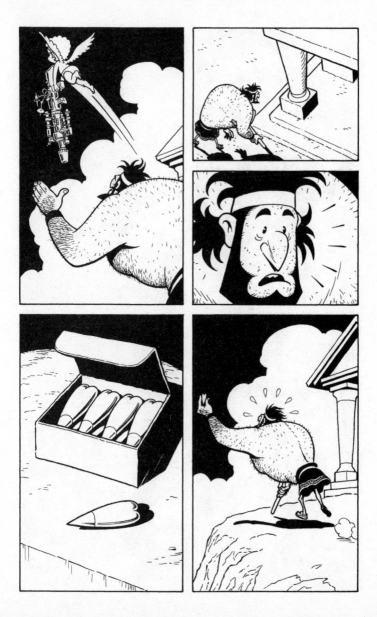

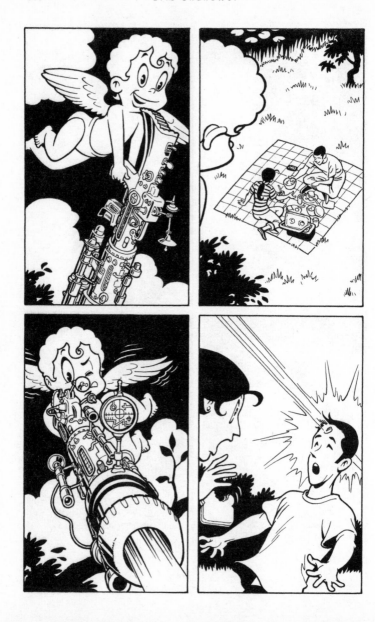

THE DRAGON

Francesca Lia Block

When they told me about the new law—that every teacher had to get the training and carry a weapon in order to teach elementary school—I thought they were insane. But then isn't the whole world in 2022? It was the strangest thing. The idea of learning to use a gun when all I wanted was to read stories about little animals to kindergartners as they sat in a circle looking up at me with wonder brightening their eyes. Clap hands and dance with them. Fill the room with colorful letters and numbers, a cozy corner for the children to snuggle in, on a beanbag chair under a paper rainbow. Some of them cried sometimes and I wiped their noses and put bandages on their skinned knees. Once we had a petting zoo in the playground. There was even one of those nearly extinct llamas with long eyelashes but he was a bit ornery so we could only look at him. On birthdays we had parades, blew bubbles, decorated cookies, and sang songs. Once there came a man who played guitar. He reminded me of Jordan with the brown of his eyes and the fullness of his mouth, and one of the little girls, Mimi, noticed I was crying at that old song "Puff, the Magic Dragon" and came over and patted at my nose with a tissue.

"Don't cry, Miss Adams, your makeup will get all runny." Her eyes loomed large behind her purple sparkling glasses, and her braids were like antennae, picking up every emotion in a room. "Are you crying because Jackie Paper came no more?"

I was crying because Jordan would come no more. Jordan is my weakness and also my great strength. I believe he saved my life.

The day it happened seemed like any day, except for the snake man. We had free-play and story time and lessons and recess. And then Terry, the young man with the reptiles, came to show them to the children. They sat in their circle around him and he took lizards out of cages for them to touch, only on the back, tentatively with one extended finger. I was worried about bites and germs, and hovered with hand wipes. Some of the lizards had been abused, Terry said in his soft voice. He had rescued them. People had starved them, burned them with cigarettes, slashed at them with knives. "Because they could." Those are the words he used. Terry then took a long, thick snake from its cage and draped it in my arms. I hid my involuntary shudders and smiled. The snake's skin had the cold, opaque whiteness of congealed milk.

While I was holding it, the young man, Terry, turned back around from slipping a lizard into its cage and pulled out his .44 Magnum. I stared down that big black dragon's maw of death.

My weapon was locked in the closet. This was a violation and I could lose my job if it was found out, but I refused to have a loaded weapon on my person while teaching babies. I refused.

People tell me even now that the whole incident proves me wrong.

But that day all I knew was that I had to save my children.

I stepped in front of them; I was still holding the white

snake. The children cowered behind me. Some were crying. I could distinguish Mimi's sniffling among them and remembered how she had held the tissue to my nose.

I said to Terry, "I'm not armed." For a moment I thought, *What if I was?* Would I have been able to use my weapon on this young man? Would I have been able to engage in a shoot-out, with the babies behind me? For a moment I thought, *You might have been wrong, Chantal.* But I knew I wasn't wrong. The weapons, that was what was wrong. All the available weapons in this world. And the lack. The lack of love.

He blinked at me with pink-rimmed eyes. I could see his hands were shaking, same as mine. But I couldn't let him see me shake.

In the morning when I pray, I breathe. After Jordan died I had to teach myself how to breathe again. Sometimes I would wake in the night thinking of him and I would forget how to take a simple breath.

"Everyone here is going to die," Terry shouted in a hollow voice, like a machine's. "You and all of them." He pointed the gun down and to my right, at the children who didn't all fit behind me. I never wished so hard that I was bigger, big as the room, my body a human shield. "All of us are going to die."

He fired.

The snake slid from my hands.

It took me a moment. It took me a moment to realize the shot had gone into the linoleum floor.

The children screamed and I only glanced back for a second to make sure they were not harmed. I could not let them see the burned-metal fear smoking through my body.

"My first name's Chantal," I said. "Chantal Adams. I'm twenty-five. I was born in Compton and I've been teaching babies for three years. How old are you, Terry?"

He didn't say a word. Only his eyes spoke loudly. But they were not looking at me, those eyes. And I knew this was bad. He was lost deep in his own head, deep in the old lizard part of his brain where killing was easy.

"You take good care of your snakes and lizards. I can see that." I tried to keep my voice calm, my body steady. I reminded myself that I had not shuddered when Terry put that snake in my arms. "Everyone needs to be taken care of."

"Everyone's going to die."

My babies. Mimi with her purple glasses and her

braid antennae. Xavier with his husky voice telling me all about trains. Taylor and Emmalee Rose, holding hands wherever they went. Barack, the smallest, shyest boy, who could read at third-grade level. After Jordan, I vowed I would never marry and have children. My students were my children. I had told myself I would always have hundreds of babies, a roomful of babies to care for and love.

I moved toward Terry and he pointed the gun at me again, straight at my face. I said, "I hear that, baby. I hear what you're saying. I understand. But it doesn't have to be this way. Life's full of pain, I know, but it doesn't have to be this way."

He lowered the gun and stared at me in silence again, back to his silence. Which was worse? The mechanical-sounding shouting or the silence?

And then it wasn't just silence.

There were sirens. His eyes zoomed around the room like trapped animals.

"Life's full of pain," I said again. There was a bitter taste in my mouth, and my ears were still ringing from the gunshot. "I had a fiancé. His name was Jordan. We were going to get married and then he died. He got cancer and died. Just twenty-one years old. How old are you, baby?

You're about that age, right?"

And then he looked at me. He looked into my eyes. He said, "I'm twenty."

"That's what I thought. Almost the same age as my fiancé was when he died. You know anyone who ever got cancer? After he passed, I wanted to die, too. I thought of ways to kill myself. I didn't want to live anymore. Is that how you're feeling, baby?"

There were voices in the hallway, and Terry glanced back over his shoulder at the door. "You haven't hurt anyone yet, sweetheart," I said. "We can work this out. This can still be okay. Let me help you."

He raised his gun again. He pointed it at the cages full of lizards. At the white snake that had slid away into the corner. At me. And the children. They were whimpering. I spread my arms out as if I could protect my babies. I thought of Jordan. We were going to get married. The theme of our wedding was going to be ancient Egypt. I was going to wear a long, pleated, white chiffon Cleopatra dress and a gold headdress and bracelets up my arm and the wedding was going to take place in a white tent shaped like a pyramid. We were going to buy a little house and never move from it, unlike my mama, who moved me almost every year to a different apartment when I was growing up. Jordan would sell homes and I would teach. We were going to have three children. He was going to coach their Little League. Someday there would be grandbabies. Jordan and I would grow old together and die in our sleep. He was not supposed to die of testicular cancer at the age of twenty-one. Shouldn't someone have found a cure by now? I was not supposed to be shot down by a gunman. These children were not supposed to die.

Terry was avoiding my eyes again. I said, "What's been going on with you, baby? What brought you here?"

He still wouldn't look at me. For a long time he didn't speak. Then he said, "I'm off my meds."

"Why's that, baby?"

He looked up and then his glance skittered away, lizard-like. He mumbled words I couldn't understand.

"What's that? I didn't hear?"

"Don't like how they make me feel."

"Yes," I said. "I understand. Do you feel better without them, though?"

He shook his head no. "I almost went somewhere else today."

"Where was that, baby?"

"To someplace that could help me," Terry said.

"You're a real good boy for trying to go get help, Terry. I can get you to a place where people can help you. If you put down that gun and let me help you, you won't get hurt."

"No one loves me," Terry said. "So why should I care about anything? Why should I give a shit?" But he was asking me. Like he really wanted an answer. And there was feeling in his voice now.

"I love you, Terry. I love you like I love all God's children. You see?" I gestured to the reptiles in their cages. "I bet you love your animals and they love you. You saved them. Someone burned that one lizard's eye out with a cigarette and you rescued him."

And then Terry turned back to me and looked into my eyes and his hands were shaking and he held out the gun in front of him. And he set down the gun.

Yes, that miracle truly occurred. Without violence, it occurred.

Just like that, he set down the gun and kicked it away from him.

"Why don't you lie down on the floor there now? And rest your head and try to breathe. I won't let them hurt you. I'll make sure that you're safe."

So Terry lay down on the floor on his stomach with his head in his hands. I didn't let my body buckle with pent-up fear, with relief, with gratitude—to God, to Jordan, to love, to whatever forces had saved me and the children. Not yet. I called Terry *baby*, and told him he was a good man for doing what he did, that he had done the right thing.

The police came in and handcuffed him and took him away. The children ran into my arms. Mimi and Xavier and Taylor and Emmalee Rose and Barack and Charlotte and Teddy and Tre and Zeke and Grace and Ivy and all the rest of them. I sobbed and shook so much I thought I'd break from it. I had not realized how afraid I was.

Instead of asking if I was okay, someone was saying to me, "Where's your weapon, Ms. Adams?" But I didn't answer.

And in its corner the white snake lay very still. And the lizards like small dragons were very still. And if dragons were real and could have wept, they would have wept with us for all the senseless deaths of little girls and boys.

THE BABYSITTERS

Jenny Hubbard

We knew why you started sneaking the dog in through the window every morning before the first school bell rang.

"This is Mary Poppins," you told us, your hand brushing the top of the dog's head. That was all the introduction we got, all the introduction we needed. We'd seen the news, read the papers, heard our moms talking to one another on the phone. We knew why she was here.

"She'll be with us for the rest of the school year," you said. "Every day." We cheered, and Mary Poppins walked around the classroom licking our hands, wagging her tail, sniffing our coat pockets for crumbs.

Mary Poppins was a pit bull with some yellow lab mixed in. Your wife had rescued her from a chain in someone's backyard two years ago, when Daisy was four. When Mary Poppins first arrived at your house, she had chosen Daisy's sunny room, Daisy's soft single bed, so you and your wife let Daisy name the dog. We knew, because you had told us, that Mary Poppins walked Daisy to the bus stop every morning and then walked herself back home again. And every afternoon at 4:00, there the dog would be, sitting at the corner, waiting for Daisy to step down from the school bus. People used to drive down your street just to see the faithful Mary Poppins at her post.

For the month after the shooting, we had a substitute teacher, Mrs. Mellinga, who didn't know anything about the history of art. Her husband coached football at the public high school. On the day of Daisy's funeral, which was private—family and close friends only—Mrs. Mellinga baked us cupcakes. "I've never been good with names," she said as we licked frosting from our fingers, "but faces? I never forget a face."

She was sitting at your desk when she told us this. We could tell she was trying hard not to look at the photograph of Daisy that we all knew was right there in front of her. Her eyelids fluttered. We thought she might cry, but she kept on talking.

"When they showed that boy who did the shooting on the news, I knew exactly where I'd seen him."

We knew where she'd seen him, too. Jeremy Tong was two years older than we were, and half a year out of high school, the school where Coach Mellinga taught. He had gone off to college in August, but he'd been kicked out for reasons that were, just now, being revealed. He'd bullied his roommate, who ended up in the psych ward. He'd erupted at a graduate teaching assistant when she handed back a test he had failed. He'd come back to town in mid-October and begun working as a dishwasher in the cafeteria where Daisy went to school.

Jeremy Tong took smoke breaks in the parking lot. On November 17, before the first bell rang, he opened fire as children began emerging from the school bus that Daisy rode. The driver was killed as she rushed down the steps to tackle the shooter. She saved many lives, but not Daisy's.

We had all met your daughter. On Veteran's Day, Daisy's school was closed, and ours was open, so she came to work with you. During our class, Daisy sat at a miniature table in the corner by the window with a pad of paper and a tray of watercolors. She wanted to know our names, and so, one by one, while you spelled them out on the whiteboard, we introduced ourselves: Marlie, Cackie, Spenser, Arielle, Caroline, and me, Julia Gray.

At the end of class, she handed out six paintings, one for each of us. Self-portraits, she told us. Each picture had a cloud in the sky with our name inside of it and, below it, a smiling girl with orange hair. Daisy had given us all her hair, which was curly and red. My self-portrait showed a girl holding hands with a tree.

Daisy looked like a child straight out of a storybook. Caroline, whose self-portrait was of a girl lying in a field of blue and purple flowers, raised her hand and said she was free to babysit on the weekends. The rest of us chimed in—we were all babysitters—and Daisy begged you to take your wife to a party so that we could come over and babysit.

"Daddy never takes Mommy on dates," Daisy told us. "It makes Mommy mad because she has a lot of cool turquoise jewelry that she never gets to wear."

This was on a Friday, and on Monday, you asked Caroline if she was free to babysit on Saturday night. She wasn't; she'd been invited to a dance by a boy she knew who went to the boarding school not far from here. You asked me next. I wasn't doing anything, so I said yes.

I imagined Daisy scooting down the stairs in footie pajamas, Mary Poppins on her heels, and on the last step. I imagined being led into the kitchen to meet your wife, a half-empty glass of wine on the granite countertop by her fingertips. I imagined that she had Daisy's hair, although your wife's was long and flowing, and that she was wearing a chunky necklace of turquoise.

I never got to babysit for Daisy, of course. None of us did, which is why we embraced Mary Poppins so obsessively, why we loved her even as she slobbered on our ballet flats, why we stole our own dogs' favorite toys and lavished them on her. We understood that it was Mary Poppins and not your wife who was keeping you tethered to your life.

There was so much we understood and yet didn't understand. When you assigned us our big project—to choose one of the famous portraits you showed us and study it and research the artist and context and place the painting on the continuum of art history—we thought at first that you were doing it for us.

I chose *Helga*, by Andrew Wyeth. Spenser chose the

da Vinci; Marlie, the Vermeer; Arielle, the Fragonard; Cackie, the Renoir; and Caroline, the Balthus. The paintings spanned the centuries and featured (arguably) the greatest portrait artists of the Western Hemisphere. At the time, that's all the connection we could see. We were juniors in high school. There were boys to love, colleges to visit, SATs to take over and over until the scores were high enough, field hockey practices to run us ragged.

To see the real connection took years of perspective.

Every time I visit one of these paintings in a museum, my fingers tremble, and I have to hold hands with myself. When you assigned us the project, you'd been searching for Daisy, not the child Daisy you knew, but the woman she would never become. By the end of the school year, you had six different Daisies, six lives she might have lived. Each portrait features a woman with red hair.

We, your girls of art history, have remained close. At our tenth high school reunion, we learned that you'd gotten divorced and moved away. We wanted to believe you were happy, that you'd found a good woman and a way to simplify your life. We wanted to believe you'd gone to Tahiti like Gauguin. We wanted to believe that Mary Poppins was still alive, still with you.

We tried to track you down on the internet but gave up as the years passed. By our twentieth reunion, we had all become mothers except for me. I'd married, but the children I have are imaginary. They are inside of the books I write and illustrate. My publisher insists that the little girls in my stories have politically correct, nondescript brown hair. But she doesn't care about the dogs. I wish I could find you, Mr. Howe. I wish I could tell you that all the dogs look like Mary Poppins, every single one of them.

THE BATTLE OF ELPHINLOAN

Elizabeth Wein

"You working, Dad?" Janet asked softly, sticking her head out the open cottage window, which was easier than opening the heavy oak-and-iron door. The smell of pipe smoke and low tide hit her in the face in a gust of wet wind off the Firth. It was a late summer morning so bright and clear that the light on the water hurt her eyes.

Struan Lennox was sitting on the narrow stone bench that was jammed up against the front wall, the lanky Scottish deerhound, Flora, sunning herself at his feet. He gave Janet a grunt that was no answer. His hands were busy holding up a heavy set of field glasses through which he was staring intently eastward toward the North Sea, and because his hands were otherwise occupied, he was using his teeth to hold his pipe. That meant his mouth was also otherwise occupied and he couldn't actually talk to his daughter.

Janet sighed. Her dad might be looking for enemy aircraft or he might be looking for a good stretch of coastline for his next painting or he might be watching birds. Any of these things could count as work if it sparked inspiration. He had a series of propaganda posters he was supposed to be designing for the Ministry of Information and he was already three submissions overdue.

The bench was the only thing that separated the cobbled Fore Street from the cottage, like every other fisherman's cottage on the harbor front. But only Janet's cottage had someone sitting in front of it in the morning. Every woman's man was away fishing, and every mother's son was off to war, barricading the island against the seemingly inevitable invasion by the German army—just as soon as they could get a toehold on some British beach, enemy troops were bound to come roaring over the water and pouring into the mainland. Big blocks of concrete had been dragged into place along the sandy spits where the Firth emptied into the North Sea to stop German tanks from unloading there.

"Dad? You got a moment? Can I take the shotgun up the cliff path? I want to get a pigeon or two."

Since the first food rationing had started early in the year, her dad had decided they'd begin as they were likely to go on, and they'd stopped buying meat. Working in propaganda had its effect on him. *We live in a fishing village, it'll mean more for everyone else, you won't miss it when it's gone,* he argued. But he didn't usually object when Janet went shooting.

Now her father grunted a question mark at her.

"They're still roosting in the old dovecote up by Elphinloan Castle. They don't belong to anybody. Lots of people get pigeons there."

Her father lowered his binoculars and turned his head to get a look at her. For a moment his set, distant expression washed fond and warm as he gave her a nod of approval; he harrumphed, and then he turned back to the potentially hostile horizon as seen through the field glasses.

"I know not to waste a shot," Janet assured him, just to make it feel like they were having a conversation. "Come on, Flora!"

She felt a bit mean inviting Flora without asking her

dad if he minded. But Janet needed the company more than he did. Sometimes Janet was pretty sure the only company Struan Lennox needed was her mother's ghost.

The cobbled lane that ran in front of the fishermen's cottages turned abruptly into a narrow path through the heather at the foot of the eroded sandstone sea cliff. The path climbed halfway up the cliff, then wound its way to the shelter of Elphinloan Point, where there was a large concrete swimming pool that filled up when the tide came in. The Home Guard had dumped bales of barbed wire all around the edge of the pool when the war started, and the concrete sunbathing terrace in front of the changing rooms now had a great big antiaircraft cannon mounted on it. Janet skirted this gun emplacement cautiously. If the soldier boys saw you, they wouldn't let you up the cliffs. Or worse, they'd only let you pass if you gave them a kiss, especially if you were up there bare-legged in last summer's too-short skirt on a sunny day. They knew Janet and liked her, but they teased her mercilessly.

There were half a dozen of them on guard today, and like Janet's dad, they were all glued to the horizon with field glasses clamped to their faces.

Something must be up, Janet thought. Maybe there's

an air raid on. She crept through the heather like a cattle rustler with tall, shaggy, unsubtle Flora trying to keep low at Janet's heels. Janet and the deerhound emerged triumphant on the open moorland at the top of the cliff path on Elphinloan Point without anyone having noticed them. It was a glorious day to be up there in the heather overlooking the glittering Firth, even without the excuse of shooting dinner.

Janet had nearly reached the wreck of Elphinloan Castle, with the black lump of the old dovecote squatting in its shadow like the castle's own strange offspring, when the attempted invasion came.

It began as a low hum, the drone of summer bumblebees. It rose and became like the relentless wing beat murmur of starlings swarming. Then the noise droned loud and mechanical, the background whine of a sawmill at work—more motor than midges, and Janet realized it was aeroplanes she could hear. She turned toward the line of high, bright cirrus in the northeast and saw the German air force, the Luftwaffe, roaring in: a swarm of Heinkel bombers and their attendant Messerschmitt fighter planes to protect them. They were only a cloud of menacing black spots high in the air above the Firth, but there were more of them than Janet could count. The whine of their approaching engines was the only sound she could hear anymore, filling the sky. She imagined the young antiaircraft gunmen on the cliff below her, hunkered in their patch of barbed wire on the sun terrace of the abandoned swimming pool, holding their breath and waiting for a good shot.

Janet wished she had her dad's field glasses.

Flora caught her excitement and danced with graceless eagerness around Janet's legs. Janet laughed.

"They're not birds, you great daftie! They're aeroplanes!" She stood straight and expectant, watching the sky, hoping to see a few of them fall. It didn't occur to her to be afraid.

The raiders roared past her, coming in lower as they lined up the railroad bridge and shipyards of Edinburgh that were their target twenty-five miles up the Firth. The dovecote and Elphinloan Castle suddenly erupted, too, in a cloud of clapping and clattering wings, as all the startled pigeons roosting in the ruined towers scattered to the skies away over the sunny moor like a flight squadron scrambling to action. Janet hurried to raise the slim Dickson shotgun to her shoulder but didn't dare fire at them—she hadn't been anticipating the shot and knew she'd miss by a mile. Flora suddenly lost her head and lolloped madly at high speed through the heather after a startled rabbit. She missed, too.

Across the Firth, another whining cloud appeared as the Royal Air Force launched its counterattack, and suddenly the cannon below the cliff exploded into havoc.

The air battle lasted ten minutes. Janet watched the silhouettes of planes reeling in the sky, the vapor trails unfurling, and the black smoke trailing behind one Messerschmitt fighter that had been hit. And then suddenly there was nothing left but the vapor trails. It was unbelievable how fast they all came and went. One minute nothing but wind and birdsong, the next all engines and gunfire, then birdsong again. It left Janet breathless.

At last she stuck her fingers in her mouth and whistled to Flora.

"Well, *that* was better than the circus!" she greeted the deerhound happily. "Come on—let's get those enemy pigeons."

She set off toward the dovecote. She might be able to nab some birds as they came back in, if they stayed together and she was patient enough to wait for them.

Janet hadn't even reached the dovecote when the wounded Messerschmitt came back.

It was flying low and now trailing smoke in three different columns of color, black and white and blue, like a stunt plane in an air show. Janet nearly wrenched her head off her shoulders as she whipped her neck backward to watch the plane scream over her head. It missed the black ruined keep of Elphinloan Castle by what looked like inches and buried itself in the heather a few hundred yards farther on across the moor.

"*Wow,*" Janet breathed.

She started to pick her way toward the downed plane. It was hard work scrambling over the tufted heather and she'd only got halfway there when the whole wreck went up in a blaze of daylight fireworks.

Janet wasn't quite close enough to feel the blast. But she was close enough to drop to her knees and clap her hands over her ears and cower on the open moor, her head buried in her arms, for longer than she could count.

The world put itself back together, as suddenly as the battle had been over. The roaring stopped. Out of the smoke on the horizon Janet saw, staggering toward her like a cadaver rising from its grave in a horror film, the looming figure of a once-human man.

He was a black silhouette in the smoke at first, but then he grew details. Not a cadaver after all, though white as a ghost beneath a trickle of gleaming liquid ruby streaming from his nose. His eyes and skull were encased in leather and isinglass. As he staggered toward Janet, he raised the back of one hand to wipe his nose and she saw the slim steely pistol clenched in his gloved fingers. His index finger was hooked against the trigger.

Flora hurtled forward in eager greeting, ridiculously anxious, as always, to welcome everybody Janet met.

On her hind legs Flora was taller than Janet. Her coat was wild and shaggy and her long snout was full of long teeth. The airman staggered back a step as the deerhound leaped at him, and in a moment of sure, defensive ruthlessness, pointed his pistol at Flora's head and fired. The crack of one clear gunshot ripped the air and Flora fell instantly.

Janet, still crouched low and having pulled her scattered wits back together after the shock of the explosion, for a moment couldn't comprehend what she'd just seen and heard.

Then her world exploded again in a storm of grief and anger. Janet stood up, pulled her dad's shotgun from her back, and pressed it to her shoulder with her wrist braced in the sling, all in one swift, thoughtless movement. But she knew, even in the maelstrom of emotion that enveloped her, that if she fired at such a large target so far away she'd never kill him. She'd no intention of wasting bird shot on him to hurt him—she wanted to kill him. So she waited for him to come closer.

But the Luftwaffe pilot didn't come straight for her. He stared down at Flora's still, lanky body for a long moment before he looked up at Janet. Then he staggered forward determinedly, holding the pistol out ahead of him in his right hand. He held his left hand open in supplication, as if he couldn't get the opposite sides of his body to agree with each other.

A split second later she realized she'd just made herself vulnerable. She'd waited too long to fire at him.

She took three deliberate steps forward, leveling the shotgun at him. She was close enough to do him a deal of damage now, but she didn't have any idea if it would be fatal damage. She didn't know if she could be sure of killing him, even up close. She had two cartridges in the shotgun and they were both full of bird shot. It was an idiotic way to try to kill anything bigger than a rabbit. But maybe he didn't know that. Her gun was about five times the size of his.

He came forward, too, still holding his pistol forward and aimed at her, still threatening.

He stopped about a yard away from her. They stood facing each other for a long moment, eyeing each other with fear and hatred.

Still training his pistol on Janet, the airman peeled off his gloves one at a time, then reached up with one hand to unbuckle the straps of his helmet and pull it off. He was younger than she'd thought. He had a round, boy's face on a hulking man's body. Not a friendly boy, though. A grim, desolate, hard-eyed stranger with a boy's round face and a bloody nose. A bullying killer who'd been knocked down and was back on his feet now.

Shoot him! Janet urged herself. *Who cares if you kill him or not? Don't shoot at his head or heart. Fill his hands or his eyes with lead shot—disable him, make him scream! Who'd blame you? He's an enemy soldier and he's just murdered the most gentle and loyal dog in the world—*

He gestured at Janet with his pistol and said something she couldn't understand. He pointed back toward the silhouette of Elphinloan Castle and the cliffs at the edge of the Firth.

Janet thought he was telling her to go.

She took a step backward. She didn't want to turn her back on him. She didn't think he'd shoot her in the back like a coward, not when he could have shot her in the face a moment ago. But she didn't want to turn and run like a coward herself, either.

Janet backed away slowly, never lowering her shotgun.

The airman followed her.

He swept his arm toward Elphinloan encouragingly, as if he wanted to urge her, *Go on! Go on!*

That's when Janet realized why he hadn't already killed her. He wanted her alive.

If she didn't shoot him now, she was going to end up as his hostage, or—

But even in her blind grief over Flora's pointless, mistaken death—adoring Flora would have never hurt *anyone*, even an invading German pilot—Janet suddenly realized that she couldn't bring herself to maim a man in cold blood because he'd killed a dog. Even Flora.

"All right, you Jerry bastard," Janet snarled aloud. "You show me what you're after. And then we'll see what we see."

She, too, gestured with one hand—an invitation.

"You can jolly well get in front of me," she told him.

He wouldn't, though. He wanted to keep an eye on her and her shotgun. He stayed at a respectful distance from her, not wanting to get in deadly range of whatever she might fire at him, but keeping her within his own sights. They walked side by side but a little apart back to the cliff path, Janet and the shot-down Luftwaffe fighter pilot, like beaters driving grouse toward a shooting party.

He made her cross the path and walk with him up past the castle to the edge of Elphinloan Point where the cliff stuck out into the Firth. Of course, he knew where to look; of course, he knew where the antiaircraft station was. He'd seen it all from the air.

Janet walked with her shotgun balanced over her shoulder. She didn't dare sling it over her back to make it easier to carry—the very thought felt like surrender. As long as she was armed, she wasn't a hostage.

The point where Elphinloan Castle stood gave spectacular views up and down the Fife coast, including the village seawall and harbor and the lighthouse on the opposite headland, and the abandoned public pool and the antiaircraft gun emplacement in between. Janet could see her own house. She couldn't see her father sitting in front of it, though. She was too far away. She wondered if Struan Lennox was still sitting on the stone bench scanning the skies with his binoculars. She wondered if he could see *her*.

She couldn't see her father, but she could see the gunners still manning the cannon on the concrete sunbathing terrace, like tiny doll figures far below across a stretch of rock and lapping water. As Janet and the German airman came close to the edge of the cliff, he hunkered down to avoid the soldiers below skylining him, and barked an order at Janet to get her to do the same.

"You must be joking!" she snarled. "What d'you take me for? They know I'm here, anyway."

But they didn't. She'd sneaked around them without them noticing her. And even if they'd noticed, they wouldn't know she was in trouble now. Janet lashed herself angrily: *Can you not put your gun to some decent use even if you can't bag a pigeon, save your faithful dog, or shoot an enemy?*

She glanced down contemptuously at the pilot now lying at her feet. Then she raised her shotgun to her shoulder and fired it once out to sea. The gunners looked up at the sound and gave Janet friendly waves.

As she raised her arm to wave back, the airman grabbed her ankle and pulled at her leg. His grip was firm and rough, and the electric shock of his hot, sweaty palm locked around Janet's bare ankle threw her off balance nearly as much as the violence of his grasp. For a moment, Janet teetered terrifyingly on the edge of the cliff. For a moment, she had a choice between throwing herself forward to escape him over the precipice or throwing herself backward into his arms.

She fell backward, still clutching the Dickson shotgun, and the German airman pulled her against him so that they were both lying on their stomachs looking over the edge. He obviously *thought* she was his hostage.

She gave him a thump on the shoulder with the stock of the shotgun and struggled free of him, hugging the Dickson under her arm so she still had control of it even if she couldn't fire it. She inched away from him a little so that he couldn't easily try to grab the gun away from her. He rubbed at his shoulder and gave her a cold, accusing stare.

"I didn't hit you very hard," Janet sneered. "You're wearing a great big jacket and it's a wee light shotgun, you great softie."

He tilted his blue-toned pistol at her as a reminder and a warning, but thank God, he didn't try to struggle with her anymore. Instead he looked away from her, gazing intently out at the landscape of the Firth spread out below him. Janet lay still on her stomach a few feet away from him. She was afraid that if she tried to get away he'd grab at her again. Wondering what to do next, Janet followed the airman's gaze out over the water.

The Firth was beautiful. She had never seen it from this angle. With her face at the cliff's edge she had no sense of being attached to the ground. It was like being a bird above the landscape, like looking at the view from the sky. Everything was in miniature: the concrete swimming pool, the harbor, the harbor wall, the lighthouse on the opposite headland, the crags of the Isle of May in the distance and the Bass Rock behind it, the blue mainland beyond. Janet wondered if the airman noticed all this beauty now or if he had noticed these things earlier, when he'd been flying over them. Or if he noticed them at all.

"D'you have a plan from here?" Janet asked the downed enemy pilot with polite sarcasm. She hated him.

The German pilot pointed at the cluster of masts down in the village harbor on the other side of the concrete tide pool. The pool was full of water; the tide was up and over the edge of the concrete rim. You could see the outline of the pool's edge beneath the water and the barbed wire the soldiers had bolted down along the rim. The concrete wall of the pool was a broad, straight, regular rectangle, faintly green beneath the film of seawater that covered it. It seemed out of place among the scattered boulders of the craggy Fife coast.

The German airman pointed at the boats in the harbor insistently, gesturing with his slim blue pistol for emphasis.

"I am not getting you a boat," Janet said hollowly.

The airman sighed and wiped his forehead. He was sweating beneath his heavy fur-and-leather jacket; the blood on his face was beginning to dry now. He looked exhausted, but not badly hurt. He wanted Janet to lead him to his escape. And unless she did something about it, he *would* eventually escape.

"If you mean to steal a boat," Janet told him, "good luck getting past the antiaircraft station."

Something in her voice made him pause. Finally he barked another query at her. She wondered how to make him understand anything she said.

He gestured again at the boats in the harbor and pointed east, toward the place where the Firth opened out into the North Sea. In one of the small sailboats or a launch, it wouldn't be impossible for a determined man to make it across to the safety of his own occupying army in Norway. With a fair wind or a motor, it would take about two days to get to Stavanger, maybe less. It would be hard work on your own. But he might get lucky and be taken on board a German patrol boat before he made land.

The Luftwaffe pilot frowned. He pointed to the boats again and drew a little path in the air with his free hand. He gave Janet a command in German and she was pretty sure what he was telling her to do.

Show me how to get around the antiaircraft station to the harbor without them seeing me.

Janet shook her head. "No. There isn't a way!"

He gave her an arch look of doubt and irony.

It was the same look her dad wore when he was on the telephone with the Ministry of Information and they were ordering him to produce some image he thought sounded ridiculous.

It was a look of disbelief that anyone could take him for such a fool.

The German airman pointed again at the tidal pool. In the time since they had come to the edge of Elphinloan Point, the tide had fallen enough to reveal the white concrete rim of the abandoned swimming pool with its garland of barbed wire shining in the sun. The water had dropped six inches in ten minutes. You could make an accurate measurement of the rate it was falling because there were depth lines painted on the outside corner of the pool.

Janet realized with dismay exactly what the pilot was thinking. If he waited here lying low for as little as two hours, he'd be able to sneak around the antiaircraft station by creeping behind the concrete wall of the pool when the tide went down.

There wasn't a thing Janet could do about the tide.

She wriggled a little farther away from the Luftwaffe pilot. She moved slowly and stayed low, aware that if she startled or angered him he might try to overpower her in a physical struggle, and the thought of rolling with him in the heather made the heat rise to her face and turned her stomach with fear. She did not want to end up pinned beneath him. It had nothing to do with being so close to the edge of the cliff.

After another few tense minutes had passed, the airman reached into his jacket and pulled out a silver cigarette case. He offered Janet a cigarette.

She stared at him in astonished disdain and shook her head.

He set down his pistol for a few moments, on the far side of his body, while he lit a cigarette for himself. Then he picked up the gun again and lay propped on his elbows on his stomach in the sun, casually smoking and watching the imperceptible fall of the tide as more and more of the concrete wall of the swimming pool slowly revealed itself.

Janet took a long, deep breath. Something rebellious in her wanted to show him she could be as casual as he. Then slowly, deliberately, she reloaded her shotgun so that she was armed with two shots instead of one. The German airman watched her with weary resignation at this ineffective defiance. He finished his cigarette. After some time he said suddenly, with clear, slow enunciation, *"Ihre Hündin. Es tut mir leid."*

Janet stared at him. He pointed over the moor, back toward the wreck of his plane. Back toward the place where he'd shot Flora.

He touched his heart gently with his hand and held it

pressed there, as if it hurt him. He repeated softly, *"Es tut mir leid."*

She guessed what he was saying. *Your hound* was clear enough even in German. The rest—

It meant, *I'm sorry.*

Whatever she'd taken him for when she first saw him staggering out of the cloud of hellfire after the explosion and the gunshot, he wasn't that anymore. He'd become human again.

And she knew he wasn't going to shoot her. Not if he was sorry about Flora.

Then Janet heard the shouts—the soldier lads from the antiaircraft station calling her name.

They'd seen her fall, right after she'd fired her gun at the sky, and the Luftwaffe pilot had pulled her off her feet, and they'd come looking for her.

Janet scrambled to her knees. She had to get a little farther away from the cliff's edge before she put up a fight, or risked yelling in response. The airman scrambled up beside her, his pistol still clutched in his big hand, pointing it now at Janet's head. She didn't believe for a second that he'd pull the trigger, but the soldier lads didn't know that.

The first of the soldiers appeared in the looming shadow of Elphinloan Castle, spotted Janet and the German pilot standing there. The soldier yelled to his companions. The other lads came running up the cliff path and across toward the cliff's edge. All of them carried rifles that could take out the engine of a dive-bomber if it flew low enough and you were a good enough shot.

The German airman was surrounded now. He had no choice but to surrender or fight alone and likely, quickly, end up dead.

Suddenly Janet didn't want any part of it. She didn't want the soldiers to kill this desperate human boy with a man's competent body in an enemy uniform, any more than she now wanted to kill him herself.

Janet put her shotgun down. She took a few steps toward her own loyal lads, the ones who'd come looking for her when they wondered or guessed what was happening to her.

Now for the first time that morning, Janet had turned her back on her enemy. She'd made a decision to trust him, but her shoulder blades still crawled with unease. Halfway to the poised, waiting solders, she turned back to look at the airman.

He was walking behind her, meekly following in her path. He still held the slim, blue-barreled pistol, but he carried it hanging at his side now, pointing earthward.

Janet held out her hand, and the airman gave her his gun.

She put that down, too.

"Thank you," said Janet. "I'm sorry also."

He nodded wearily and walked at her side into the waiting circle of the enemy.

DARK HOBBY

Edward Averett

In another life, Swayzee might be popular, handsome, well liked. Might arrange his accomplishments on a shelf above his dresser so they could be the last things he sees before the lights go out at night. Instead of that bottle of medicine. In another life.

But *this* is his life. He stands outside the back door and places the flat of his tongue against the rusty metal mesh of the screen just to see what it feels like. It is cold and shocking.

He's in the middle of a fight with himself but can't take a side. The sweet corner of his brain fights with the sour.

Tell Grams, sour. *Don't tell her,* sweet.

Tall and thin like a clothespin, he slaps the side of his head and paces along the porch. Slap one side. *Yes.* Slap the other. *No.* No talent up there for making any big decision, so they say at school. Not much talent anywhere that can be measured in the regular ways.

He finds her in the kitchen, the radio playing country music, a big pot of chili on the stove, a big scowl on her face. "You been up there?" she asks. He watches her old jowls jiggle, plays dumb so she'll ask again and he can watch them some more. He guesses she has gained maybe twenty pounds.

"Nothing up there," he says. "Not a damn sign of her."

"Watch that mouth." She waits an instant, has his attention. "You're not too big to send away, too."

This is minor for her, easier than his rushes of mayhem; the way his personal electricity jumps the wires sometimes. He stares her down. She stares back. The two of them locked in an embrace not of their own making. It's as if she is telling him, *Can't you do something about this life of mine?* She figures he can't, but that is the lie she tells herself. He knows there is a witch called guilt that sleeps in her heart. Every once in a while the witch wakes up and accuses her of sending her only daughter away. He

can see the picture she makes in her head of herself standing on the front porch while Gramps folds his arms across
his chest and forbids Swayzee's mother to ever come back.
The guilt witch hatched in her heart when Grams didn't
say a thing and has eaten most of it away since.

His mother being sent away probably wouldn't matter
much except for what happened later. It's seven big years
now since the air balloon in her veins. He sometimes
stands in the upstairs bathroom with his shirt off and
underpants tied in a tourniquet around his upper arm.
His undisciplined penis pushes against the cold porcelain
of the sink. He pretends to sink a needle into the crook of
his elbow, like Gramps described it.

*She took a damn needle, filled the thing with nothing
but the air we breathe. Then jabbed a hole till the blood
swirled in the syringe. Plunged it home.*

Afraid of things sharp, Swayzee uses the handle of a
toothbrush.

*Pop. Her brain went bald, then grew fingerlets of blood.
Cut off her thinking. Dried out her heart. Do not ever,
Swayzee, do not ever put air in your veins. There are other
ways to accomplish things. Whaddya think I taught you
how to aim for?* Gramps is old old and was in the Pacific

Theater so he should know.

Now Grams wins the stare contest. She can do it till her eyeballs grow tacky. "She's up and had them, hasn't she?"

"Think so," he replies.

A quiver at the corner of her lips. What keeps her heart beating is a mystery to everyone. After all, she doesn't like Gramps. Throws food down in front of him like he is a nonpaying customer. Doesn't use the pre-spot remover on his clothes, so he sits on special occasions at the VFW with his Purple Heart and coins of grease decorating his shirts. Swayzee is a burden to her. She squeezes lemons over his open wounds. She curses the important people on the TV. Curses the school administration.

"Don't even know what that means," she says to them. "Speak English."

"We can accommodate him, but let's not set our expectations too high."

Grams harrumphs. "Well, he ain't retarded. Boy could shoot an apple off the top of your flat head."

How many times has the palm of her hand brushed her forehead in frustration? By now, the world owes her a living, but this is not living.

From out of the radio, Swayzee hears this: "There is no good life that doesn't have a few dark hobbies."

This was from Gramps back when he could finish his sentences strong: *Secret of life. Never let 'em know even the smell of your sweat. Just show 'em what you can do.*

He follows her up the hill toward the barn. He can barely keep up. She seems to like this part. He speeds up and tries to pass her, but catches a swinging elbow. He falls into the drying black walnut leaves.

"Get up," she commands. "You got to show me."

"I need to wax my shoes," he says.

She looks up at the sky, framed by the dark arterial limbs of the trees. It is cold, but she hasn't noticed till now. They speak in smoke signals. "There'll be a deep freeze tonight." She reaches down and yanks him up by the arm. "Come on. This ain't the only thing I got to do today."

They are in the barn that actually used to be a small house. Sometimes Swayzee pretends it's still a real home. Chickens lay eggs in the sink. They roost and shit in the master bedroom. Gramps once removed the testicles of a jersey bull in the living room. Down the hallway toward the bathroom is where she heads. She's given up on Sway-zee. But it doesn't matter: her ears are like a dog's, and the calico is blowing the silent whistle. She stands in front of the shower with her hands on her hips. Swayzee pokes his head inside her elbow. He sees a writhing, maggoty ball of new kittens. The calico looks up at them. Her lips move but only Swayzee can see and hear. *Put some air in my veins, why don't you?*

"Fetch a gunnysack."

Off he goes. *He'll make a good soldier,* Gramps used to say. *Good at following directions. Fastest in his class, I'll bet. Took him what, two minutes to get it put together and loaded right?* He searches the baby's room for the old grain sacks but can't find what she wants. He pulls away the bale of hay with his big hand then tugs on the cord that lifts up the secret door. He swoons for a moment. Sees them all lined up like sardines in the cans he and Gramps eat from. Bullets. One by one, he's filled up this space. Little by little. Stolen from behind the cedar chest. From the box under the old magazines in the cellar. They seem to fall from the sky, and Swayzee holds out his hands in supplication as he collects them all and hides them away in this hole. He closes the trapdoor, shoves the bale back over, and returns to her.

"No gunnysacks there," he says.

She doesn't believe him. "Bring me a sack. I don't care what it is." The calico's lips move again, but Swayzee slaps his hands over his ears so he can only hear it deep in his brain. *Let me keep one little girl,* it says. *The one that looks like me.*

He drags back a big, thick paper grain sack. He wants to stay, but she pushes at him. "Go do your job," she says. "Go on."

He's down the hill again. Her herb garden is surrounded by the stones she needs. He selects two smooth, freckled ones and hefts them in each hand. Now the border of her garden looks like a boxer's mouth with a couple of teeth knocked out. He looks up and sees her coming down the hill. She throttles the top of the bag like the neck of a goose. Behind her, the calico trails. She squats and cries, then runs to catch up.

Grams takes the two stones from Swayzee and carefully lays them at the bottom of the bag, next to the struggling kittens. Then she holds the neck between her legs and ties it with twine.

"There you have it," she says, throwing her hands in

the air like she's just won the calf-roping competition.

Gravely, she picks up the bag and heads down the curving driveway. She stops before her head disappears. "You coming?" The calico turns and asks the same.

But he doesn't. He runs in the house and up the stairs. Taped on his bedroom door is his proudest accomplishment. It says:

KNOW THY GUN
KNOW THY SELF

And below it:

SWAYZEE MORRISON HAS SATISFIED
ALL THE REQUIREMENTS FOR GUN SAFETY.

"Proud of you," Grams said when they taped it up. "Smarter than they all think you are."

Now he opens the window and rests his elbows on the sill. From there, he sees her come out of the trees and stand before the pond down by the well house. He has the toothbrush in one hand and depresses the cylinder as down below she twirls the sack and tosses it out toward the middle. Just before it hits, the sack tears and the rocks and the kittens tumble out making separate splashes in the thin ice of the pond. The calico runs to the edge and pads out on the thick shore ice. Her kittens pop up and work their paws frantically against the surface. Grams bends down and picks up pebbles. If a kitten moves toward shore, she lobs a pebble in the water, and is remarkably accurate as she hits them, driving them back. Even from way down below, Swayzee thinks he can hear Grams: *I am so unhappy to have to do this.* Lately he is sure he can hear the same coming from the kids in his classes. *We are so unhappy.*

Now Swayzee runs into the old bedroom. He knows that if he pushes the cedar chest away from the wall, he'll find the rifle. He picks it up. A 30-06. Its bullets are like missiles. In the drawer on Gramps's side of the bed he pulls out the rag and the oil. He sits on the bed and rubs and rubs at the stock, minute after minute until it shines. He picks it up and sights it in, over toward the door. This is it. When the big comes into his bones and his meat. It feels like the cool smooth inside of Elaine Sandeborn's leg when the kids at school tricked him and then everybody jumped out and laughed him down the stairs.

He sat once in the counselor's office and listened as they talked. *Can't blame him for not knowing the appropriate rules for dating. We'll work on it with him. Meantime, keep him where he is. He mostly gets along just fine. Just has to stay away from Elaine.*

"He's passed the exam for his carry permit," Grams said. "Not stupid, this boy. Just troubled. You ask me, you should be taking a look at those other kids."

Grams is back and now steps into the doorway from the hall and right into Swayzee's line of sight. Her body sags when she sees the rifle pointed at her. One day she will just crumple from all this heavy life. He sees a new scared look on her for an instant. But just for an instant. It tickles him. It touches the sweet part of his brain. He smiles everywhere but on his lips.

"Put that thing down!" she orders. And all the big deflates as she yanks it from his grasp by the barrel. "Gramps will flay the meat off your bones."

He knows Gramps wouldn't. Can't. But Gramps would be proud. Even prouder if he knew that Swayzee's been practicing what Gramps preaches about war. But it's Grams and he falls to his knees. Begs for her forgiveness. Plays like he's on the stage so they won't know the truth. There is a great fetid pool he tells no one about. Not Grams, not the perfect lady at the clinic where he can spend hours watching the curl in her hair. In the pool, he sees his long-lost older sister and his father. Both refugees who took a boat to some other life. Left Swayzee without a map to find them. Didn't tell him that you can be smart as a whip and still nobody likes you. Pretty girls crush themselves against the sides of this pool, hoping you won't touch them. He imagines his sister and his father swim around in their own better pool called luck like a couple of kittens with life preservers. Getting somewhere, not like Swayzee. He doesn't tell anybody about the other one who lives in his pool. Grams has her witch . . . well, Swayzee has one better. His voice is everywhere. But quiet. *They don't know*, he whispers. Gramps would like him. They say the same things.

He goes upstairs, pulls his oxfords from under the bed. Takes the rectangle of paraffin hidden inside one. He goes back down and plops himself on the hassock next to Gramps. No money for skates again this year so he must work on the shoes. Gramps sits in his wheelchair, a beam of winter sun cooking his face. Swayzee turns one shoe upside down and runs the paraffin across the sole. Back and forth and back and forth. A nice waxy buildup. While he does this, he talks to Gramps. And Gramps answers back. Not to anyone else for ten years since the stroke, but to Swayzee he does.

The inside of your head is a delicate thing. Your skull, now, it's made to protect your brain from the outside. But God didn't make anything to protect your brain from the inside. See there? That's the rub. All the while you're slogging along, looking for the enemy out in the jungle, and bam, there he is, sneaking up on you from the inside. In war, everybody's the enemy and believe you me, we both know it's a war out there for you, Swayzee. Be careful. Be ready. I saw plenty of that sneaking in the Pacific Theater.

Swayzee reaches out and touches the wheelchair. He hopes one day to get a part on the stage of the Pacific Theater. He might stand up before the audience and say, "No, you cannot take those medications. They are extremely bad for you. They make it all sour and you can't taste anything. They make it hard to sight in the gun. Hard to do a double Salchow. I will show you how not to take them."

Grams is so unhappy, mute Gramps says.

He brings the shoe up to his nose and sniffs. His

tongue comes out and licks the heel. Just like the top of a jar of blackberry jam. He will be ready.

A few days later, it is worth the wait. It is colder outside. The leaves have all deserted the trees. Grams is busy in the barn. Swayzee puts on his sweatshirt, now heavy with the little missiles. He uses his silent skills to slip into the old bedroom. Moves the chest, pulls out the gun. He slings it on his back and it is like a part of his spine: a part that holds his body straight and true.

He winds down the driveway to the pond. He lays the rifle in the ivy and sits back on the gravel and trades his boots for his oxfords. They are shiny and black. He can see the whole world in the leather. He racks the rifle back on his spine and tiptoes through the dead grass and onto the ice. It creaks under his weight. He likes the sound. The ice is practically the only thing that speaks nicely to him. Then he glides across the ice and around the little islands of broken cattails poking up. The wax has made him a star. He twirls and jumps and spreads his arms wide while behind him the rifle is safe and sound, like the biathlon sport he's seen in the Winter Olympics.

As he moves so gracefully, he can hear his fans.

Swayzee! Swayzee! We love you, kid!

He pumps his arms and gets his speed up. Leaves his sour brain way behind. If he skates fast enough, he can catch up to all the ones who left him. He leaps into the air and thumbs a ride on a normal wind and spins and twirls and rotates. He laughs and screams and introduces himself to all the pretty girls. Then he lands solidly, perfectly, and stops himself with the toe of his oxford.

Yeah, Swayzee, old buddy, old pal! You're the best!

He skates from one end of the pond to the other and back again. It is a competition that Swayzee always wins. He skates out to the middle. He knows it is the deepest here. Over everybody's head. Deep as the pit in his brain that everyone thinks is empty but really isn't. The swirling cold from the north has made it thicker here than it was just last week. It is here where he has perfected his best moves. And it is here that he makes his mistake.

He tries to push off to get his speed going fast enough to twirl himself up into space, but he catches on one of the islands of cattails and falls hard, face-first onto the shimmering ice. The gun goes off and a bullet speeds straight and true into the trunk of a young naked maple. His nose slams into the ice and the pain paints its bright notice behind his eyes. He yowls and slips and slides on his blood that is fast congealing. A front tooth is rocking in its socket. He falls again on his cheek.

Something stares up at him and he tries to focus. Something there locked in the ice. A dark blue eye, a swatch of calico. As the blood spatters from his nose, he clambers up onto his hands and knees. He peers down.

Locked in there but moving its mouth. Swayzee can hear it. *I'm the one who looks like her.*

He wails and scrambles to stand up. The blood falls freely. His jacket is splotched and stiffening. He screams and screams. He stumbles, splays his legs, falls forward across the ice to the shore. He finds the ground and runs. Who cares about the ought-six? Who cares about his oxfords? Who cares? They propel him up the hill in a frenzy of blood and grief and a feeling that some bad things never end.

He can't tell her well enough. Can't get it past the blood. "Alive!" he finally gabbles. "Alive!"

Grams is puzzled. She tries to staunch the blood but he won't let her. She looks at him and her breath pulls back. Who is this man she now sees in his eyes? She fidgets. "Don't try it, boy," she says.

"But it's alive," he says.

"Who? Where?"

He leads her down the driveway, no time to put on her heavy coat and scarf. He yanks her along. She doesn't care about the blood right now. She doesn't say a word about the rifle strapped to his back. At the pond, he refuses to go out on the ice again, but points it out to her.

"She's alive!" he shouts. "Alive!"

She glances down at his scuffed oxfords. She tears a piece of her sleeve off and jams it next to his nostrils, makes him hold it there. Then she walks out on the ice.

It crackles beneath her, making great ancient sounds. She's gained twenty pounds this year and that, plus the weight of her world, is finally too much. She looks down and, through the slushy blood, sees the kitten trapped in the ice. Sees the one dark blue eye observing her. It is the eye that will not let her go, the one unblinking reminder that maybe it was a mistake to walk out here.

She turns and looks at her grandson as the ice buckles and then breaks beneath her. She goes down quickly, inevitably. She comes up and spits the frigid murky water from her mouth. She clutches for the edge of the ice, but it breaks away from her grasp. Down once more, this time the cold is dragging her, sopping into her dress, into her socks, filling the airy spaces of her shoes.

Rising again, "Swayzee!" she calls. "Swayzee! Help!"

But what she sees is Swayzee calmly collecting stones from the driveway and as she battles the cracking ice, he lobs them, one by one out to the middle of the pond. One hits in the open water. One hits the solid ice and skates across and catches her on her heavy lips.

"Swayzee!" she calls a final time before she goes under yet again.

I was so unhappy, he hears her say from beneath the water.

Swayzee pauses. The pebbles are cold in his palm. He waits. It is quiet. The ice has stopped its awful wailing. He knows what will happen next and he quickly pulls the rifle from his back and fixes on the hole Grams has made. In a few seconds comes his reward. The little witch bobs to the surface, puffing, crying, those wicked little teeth chomping at the water. She is looking to come for Swayzee. He knows better. He butts the rifle against his shoulder and catches her through the sight. He fires and the happy bullet hits the mark.

"Yes," says Swayzee. The big is back. His bones grow.

His meat grows. They feed the illustrations of success in his brain.

Yes, you can do it, Swayzee, old boy, old pal.

He likes this part. Knowing that he can finally make something of himself. So many witches to keep from shore. Keep out of people's hearts. Now that the witch has gone under, everything is quiet again.

He wants to leave. Wants to go back up and see what Gramps has to say about what he's done. He turns and nearly trips over the calico sitting next to his boots. They share a glance. There is much for them to talk about.

Who's next? says the cat. *How about that Elaine Sandeborn?*

Guys won't chase me down the stairs this time.

Up to the barn then?

To that hole in the floor.

There is the tiniest quiver at the corner of the calico's mouth. Then she turns and twitches her tail as they go up the driveway together. Swayzee sticks out his tongue. The air is a shock and it tastes so much sweeter.

THE GUNSLINGER

Peter Johnson

The black Mazda reeked of cigarettes and fear.

The cigarettes were Maura's mother's. The fear was hers.

She turned the key, and the engine coughed itself awake. The afternoon was still hot and sunlight flashed off the hood.

Maura was going to buy a gun.

She knew nothing about guns, though they were a daily threat in Gabby's neighborhood. Just last summer, Gabby had told Maura how a carload of boys had peppered her housing project with bullets while neighbors sat outside barbecuing and making small talk. Gabby also said she knew where to get a gun if she felt unsafe, which was why Maura was picking her up.

It was a short drive to the Dunkin' Donuts located at the end of the strip mall. Maura could see Gabby standing on the corner, yelling at two guys in a yellow Mustang convertible. She wore skintight jeans and a snug, white sleeveless top. Her dark curly hair was drawn back into a ponytail. She was tall and thin, her body sculpted from exercise and weight training. She was a sprinter. That's how she and Maura had met last summer. Gabby did the 100- and 200-yard dashes, and Maura ran long distance. Neither one of them had the money to afford a premier track camp in the city, but their coaches finagled them scholarships. They saw each other daily for four weeks that summer and kept in touch through Facebook, sometimes meeting at the mall for lunch.

Maura pulled up behind the Mustang. When Gabby saw her, she shot the guys in the car the finger. They laughed, and one called her a slut. Then they peeled away.

"Slut, my ass," Gabby said, sliding into the front seat of the Mazda.

Maura laughed.

"It ain't funny, girl," Gabby said. "Dumb boys think every beautiful black girl has the morals of a rap diva. I'm a straight-A student on the fast track to something big."

There was no doubt in Maura's mind that was true.

She was about to pull away when Gabby grabbed her by the forearm. "Why did you scrub yourself down, girl?"

"What?" Maura asked.

"No makeup. You look like a nun."

Maura felt herself smile, and that was nice, since for the last few weeks she'd been so depressed she'd had trouble getting out of bed. And as for makeup, the truth was, she didn't want to look pretty anymore.

"Don't worry about today," Gabby said. "These guys will want your money, and then we're gone. They don't need to know nothin'. You understand?"

Maura nodded.

"No need to share. You need protection, right?"

Maura nodded again.

"You're not going to do anything stupid, right?"

"No," Maura said.

Alex didn't think much about it when he first saw Maura at the mall. He needed new desert boots. They were a hundred and fifty dollars, but he needed them. They were cool, so his mother gave him the money. It was nice to be able to spend money like this, and not have to work crappy summer jobs to buy clothes. Instead he had time to get in shape for football.

As he was leaving the shoe store, he saw her sitting in the food court on a bench by a water fountain. Looking at him. Not waving or approaching. Just staring. He waved but she didn't respond, so he kept walking toward J.Crew. He needed new shorts and some T-shirts. He needed some kind of lightweight pants.

It was after he left J.Crew that he saw her a second time, squatting on another bench across from the store. Now this was getting annoying.

She actually looked good. She wore white short shorts and a blue sleeveless knit top, her long brown hair breaking across her breasts. She had one leg crossed over the other. She had nice legs. He had remembered that, and also the green pendant that hung around her neck. That night, he had retrieved it from the floor and slid it into her pocket. That was nice of him, thoughtful.

But this was creeping him out.

He decided to talk to her.

"What's up?" he said.

She kept staring at him. She looked a little stoned.

"Okay," he said. "If that's the way you want it, I'm cool with that."

Still no response.

She looked sad, then angry, then sad.

"I gotta go," he said. "But let's talk sometime, okay?"

He was about to leave when she said something very softly.

"What?" he said.

"I said, 'Why?'"

Now *this* was awkward.

"Like I said, Maura, let's get together. Some place quiet. But I have stuff to do now. I'll call, okay?"

Still no answer, so he smiled and headed toward the sunglasses kiosk. That was the last item he needed to buy.

He didn't see her again until after he paid for parking and headed through the steamy underground garage toward his red Audi. He wanted to get home, then go to the country club for a quick dip. Dory said she'd be there around three. Dory was hot, and as far he knew, no one had gotten with her.

He placed a few bags on the hood while he opened the door. When he went to retrieve them, he spotted her. She was leaning against a concrete pillar.

This was too much now. He tossed the bags into the backseat. He was going to confront her, say it was creepy to stalk him like this. She had everything all wrong. If it hadn't been for him, she would've been in real trouble.

He looked for her again, wanting to set things straight, but she was gone.

Maura was surprised where she and Gabby had ended up. She had expected a run-down project. Instead, interspersed among yellow-brick three-story apartment complexes, were a number of well-kept two-family homes. Maura wouldn't have chosen to walk there alone at midnight, but now, at four p.m., kids were playing street soccer, and a gray-haired black man was smoking a pipe on a front porch.

"I thought you said you lived in the ghetto."

"Well, it ain't exactly Beverly Hills," Gabby said. "Just remember, these boys will try to spook you, so ignore them. You've got the money, right?"

"Yeah," Maura said.

Gabby led her up the porch stairs of a white two-family and knocked once on the door before entering. Maura followed, expecting someone to yell at them, but nothing happened.

There were four boys about Maura's age. Two were on the floor playing a video game. On a couch, a black kid waved to Gabby. He was sketching the two video players on lined pages of a spiral notebook. Beside him was a white kid with close-cut blond hair. He was shirtless and heavily muscled, and next to him was a shoe box.

They all stopped to look at the girls. They looked hungry. They looked like they wanted to have fun.

The shirtless kid stood and smiled at Maura. He was handsome. "Thanks for coming," he said.

The black kid was up in an instant. "I'll do the welcoming," he said, then jokingly bowed toward Maura.

"This is my cousin, Rashim," Gabby said. "This is his house."

"You girls want anything to drink?" Rashim said.

Maura felt her chest tighten, but she couldn't leave now. This was something she had to do.

"Just give us the gun and we'll be on our way," Gabby said.

"And you used to be so much fun, cousin," Rashim said.

"I was never fun like that."

"Like what?"

"Like what you mean."

The shirtless kid approached. He knew he had a nice body. "No time like the present," he said.

Maura was having trouble breathing again, but Gabby was calm. "The gun, Rashim, now, or I'll tell your mama the nasty things you've been up to." She laughed.

"The money first," Rashim said, so Maura got the hundred dollars from her purse and handed it to him.

The shirtless guy opened the shoe box and removed a gun. It was smaller than Maura would've thought. Her first inclination was to run, but then she remembered why she was there.

The shirtless guy surprised everyone by pointing the gun at the two girls.

"Get that outta my face," Gabby said.

"It's not loaded," he said. "The bullets are in the box. There are only five of them." He looked at Maura. "You aim to shoot someone?"

"No, just scare him."

Maura could feel Gabby staring at her. She hadn't exactly told Gabby the truth.

"How does it work?" Maura asked.

All the boys laughed, and the shirtless one said, "You point it at someone and pull the trigger."

"I just want to scare him," she repeated.

"Yeah," one of the kids on the couch said, "but then something goes wrong. I once shot a dude in the hand. It was a mistake."

"Yeah, a mistake," Rashim said, and they all laughed again.

"Here," the shirtless kid said, "hold it."

Reluctantly, Maura took the gun, surprised at how light it was. Suddenly she wasn't so afraid. She felt as if she had done this before, maybe as a kid. Maybe she had held a toy gun, and it was as simple as that. Maybe she wouldn't even have to put bullets in it. After a few seconds, it felt warm in her hands.

"That's enough," Gabby said, looking curiously at Maura. She took the gun from her and returned it to the box. "We're outta here."

Everything would have been fine but one of the kids from the floor began to circle them. Then the shirtless guy did the same, poking Maura in the ribs and saying, "Time to party."

Maura remembered another room, a girl's bedroom, but not hers.

She looked at the box with the gun in it, but Gabby got there first, wedging the box under her arm. "You wannabe gangsta boys don't scare us," she said.

"Hey, hey," the shirtless guy said. "That kind of talk won't do." He was mad now. He was going to do something stupid. That's what guys did when they were mad.

Rashim got in the kid's face. "Chill out," he said, and then to Gabby, "Just scat, girl."

"You really going to let 'em go?" the shirtless kid said.

"She's family," Rashim said. And that reminder seemed to calm everyone.

In the car Gabby said, "Who you going to scare? You said your mama's boyfriend's been hassling you. You said you were afraid of what he'd do next."

Maura had lied about the boyfriend.

"Does it matter?" is all she could say.

"Sure does," Gabby said. "I don't want you shooting up your school or something crazy like that. Don't make me sorry for helping you."

"I won't," Maura said.

"Promise?"

"Promise."

* * *

To Alex she was one of those kids you go through school never noticing. Not a geek or an outsider. Just a quiet presence, the girl barely visible at the edge of the class photo, too polite to push her way to the front. There was something sexy about that kind of reserve, so when Josh pointed her out, it got Alex thinking.

"Something's changing with that girl," Josh had said.

"What girl?"

"The one by the water fountain," Josh said. "I think her name's Laura or Maura, something like that. Really nice legs, but I don't remember her ever wearing a skirt that short. I'm a leg man, so it's something that would've registered."

The girl was sipping from the fountain, and Alex had to agree about the legs.

"Definitely a possible notch on the Gunslinger's holster," Josh said.

That's what Alex's friends jokingly called him, "The Gunslinger." He thought it was a stupid name, though it was cool to have that reputation, even if it was exaggerated. At first he thought girls would shy away when they heard about it, but just the opposite seemed to be happening, so he felt obliged to live up to it. And that's partly why he approached the girl at the fountain.

When she turned, he startled her. She dropped a book onto the floor, and he retrieved it. She blushed and that's when he knew it was a done deal. Just a question of how to handle it.

"Sorry," he said, smiling. "I'm clumsy by nature."

"Not what I'd expect from a jock," she said.

So she has some spunk, Alex thought. *I like that.* He looked closely at her. She was actually pretty cute but, for some reason, just missed being hot. Was it her nose? Her mouth? Were her eyes too close or far apart? He couldn't put his finger on it.

"You make it sound like a disease," Alex said.

"If I thought that, I wouldn't be running track."

That's where I saw her, Alex thought, remembering how the cross-country team practiced on the track circling the football field.

And so they chatted, followed by their first date at the pizzeria, some more talk about school and the plans she had for the future. The usual stuff Alex had to listen to, knowing he had to go slow with this girl. A few more dates, and then they'd go to his cousin Henry's party. It was in another town. Most of the kids would be from

Henry's private school, and Henry's parents would be in Europe, so they'd have the house to themselves.

On the third date, he kissed her, not hard, teasing her with his tongue to see what she knew, which wasn't much. He never touched her while they kissed, just leaned in innocently, not wanting to scare her off. It was nice, and for a moment, he wondered if he might end up liking this girl. She was different, inexperienced but a little feisty, too. He learned a lot about her: that her father had split, that she thought her mother was prettier than she was (which turned out to be true), and that they were having a tough time financially. The more he learned, the more he realized how unhappy she was.

He felt strangely sad and exhilarated by this knowledge. So he asked her to Henry's party, and she said yes. He told her to bring her bathing suit, and he promised her mother she'd be back by midnight. He did all the right things. He gave her mother Henry's address and also his own parents' phone numbers, knowing she'd never follow up on these things.

So everything was set. What made it even better was that he was looking forward to the party. He was beginning to like this girl named Maura.

* * *

The shirtless kid was right: there were only five bullets. Maura laid them out on her bed in the shape of a fan, like the silver-painted fingernails of an imaginary hand. Gabby had shown her how to slide the cartridges into the chamber. Although Maura didn't plan on shooting the gun, she practiced inserting and removing the bullets. She felt comfortable holding it when the cylinders were empty, but when full, the weapon seemed heavier, as if weighted down by the possibility of death. She held it away at arm's length, her hand uncontrollably shaking, which, in a way, was reassuring. It made her realize she could never actually shoot anyone. She stared at the gun, still amazed at how easy it was to purchase.

At one point, she decided to remove all but one bullet. She imagined standing over Alex, spinning the chamber, playing Russian roulette. She pictured him begging her to stop, just as she had. She was about to remove the last bullet when she heard a knock. It was her mother, calling her for dinner. Before opening the door, she placed the gun in the box and slid it under her bed.

After dinner, back in her room, Maura thought about yesterday afternoon. Why had she followed him to the mall? How pathetic! How just like her to cower in the distance instead of confronting him. Wouldn't she ever change?

She had friends. She was athletic, and no one could say she was ugly, but she always knew her chances of becoming one of the cool kids—the ones that seemed so confident, so unafraid—were slim to none. She was pretty but not pretty enough. Funny, even witty at times, but too easily hurt. And when that happened, she'd withdraw rather than fight. Added to these deficiencies was the fact she had an AWOL father, and a mother who always struggled to make ends meet, dating divorced guys who never stayed with her.

Consequently Maura was surprised when Alex had asked her out, even more surprised that he was nice. She knew his reputation, but her girlfriends were wrong. She had been kissed by different boys, and Alex's kisses were sincere. Any other guy would've pushed for more.

She even felt comfortable telling him about her father and admitting she was jealous of her mother's beauty, and that, secretly, she thought her mother had driven her father away.

So how did she end up at a lousy mall, stalking him,

able to mumble only one word, "Why?"

He probably laughed all the way home. She could almost hear that laugh, along with the laughter of the other boys, the ones at Rashim's house and at the party. Those memories frightened her, but she wasn't going to be scared anymore.

Alex was.

If Alex were ever on trial, and he sometimes worried Maura might bring it to that, this is what he would say.

First, he was fond of her. He wasn't a creep. He took only what was offered. What did Maura think they were going to do at an unsupervised party? Hold hands? Up until then, he had never groped or talked dirty to her, but it was only natural to take it to the next level.

It was about 90 degrees that early June night, and everyone was drinking or smoking dope. He was surprised at how well Maura fit in, almost proud to be with her. Early on, she didn't drink, but then someone handed her a rum and Coke, and she liked it. He told her to take it easy. These weren't your normal rum and Cokes—more like glasses of rum with a shot of Coke. But Maura kept downing them, becoming more relaxed and talkative.

That's when he realized his night might get more interesting if the drinks kept coming, so he mixed them himself.

But then she got a bit aggressive, making fun of the gunslinger thing, and that pissed him off. So he led her to the greenhouse, wanting to make clear who was in charge. He started to kiss her hard, and she pushed him away a few times, so he slowed down until he regained her trust. A few minutes later, he steered her out of the greenhouse, through a throng of partygoers, toward the main house, finally ending up in Henry's sister's bedroom.

Things were looking good until she said she wanted to go home, and that didn't seem quite fair. Rather than get mad, he was smart enough to back off. He'd been through this before. He coaxed her onto the bed and began kissing her gently, the way he had on previous dates. She seemed content with this, so he got more aggressive. At first she responded in kind, and then something unexpected happened. She started to nod off, so he had to push the issue, jostling her awake. She fought a little but, eventually, they got it on. Although she asked him to stop a few times, she never screamed or hit him, so he took his time.

Afterward, she drifted off, and while he was getting dressed, Henry and two other guys barged in.

"Whoops," Henry said.

Then one of Henry's friends saw Maura and said, "Let's party," which made them laugh.

"Leave her alone," Alex said.

"Well, *you* certainly didn't," Henry said.

Alex got in between them and Maura.

"You'd actually get your ass kicked for her?" Henry said.

"She's totally wasted," Alex said.

"We can see that," Henry replied.

Then another one of Henry's friends, a guy who looked like he might have played football, said, "This is too messed up, Henry. Let's go downstairs."

Henry pondered that for a few moments, then they all left.

Alex shook Maura awake as best he could and helped her to get dressed. He saw her pendant on the floor and slid it into the front pocket of her jeans. She was having trouble walking, so he guided her downstairs and then to his car.

A little later, after she had puked a few times, they were parked outside a Dunkin' Donuts. Alex had bought her a muffin and a large black coffee. He kept asking if she was okay, but she wouldn't answer. Instead she stared out the passenger-side window like a zombie.

He got her home by midnight, just as he had promised.

He was relieved.

It had been a very long night.

Maura had never been drunk before. But she liked these rum and Cokes. She knew she was high but wasn't concerned. If anything, she felt more like herself, thinking she might slip into her bathing suit. She wandered around the pool, laughing at silly jokes, surprising herself by flirting. She even poked fun at Alex's reputation as a gunslinger. That wasn't nice, but what an insanely stupid nickname.

Still, Alex was hot, every girl at school knew that, and he'd been nice to her, so she had no problems trailing him to the greenhouse. They started to make out, though this time it was different. He seemed angry and acted more like he wanted to wrestle than to kiss. And this scared her, so she said no. But then he became the Alex she knew, so she gave in, even agreeing to follow him to the main house. She finished her fifth rum and Coke on the way, and that's when the real buzz arrived. The splashing and laughter around her seemed amplified, and the glaring floodlights above the pool made her see spots.

Alex squeezed her hand and led her to Henry's house, then upstairs to a bedroom. It had to be a girl's bedroom because it had a huge canopied bed with a soft pink comforter and pink pillowcases. On the dresser were what looked like old music boxes. She was about to examine one when Alex pushed her onto the bed.

"No," she said. "I'm really out of it."

"So am I," he said.

He started to kiss her, but something didn't seem right. She felt woozy and very, very tired. *Who falls asleep when they're kissing someone?* she thought.

"I want to go home," she said.

But he ignored her, trying to unbutton her blouse and unzip her jeans.

She pushed him away, but he kept at it.

"No," she said very loudly.

"Jeez, Maura, calm down."

She should have yelled at him then, but the five rum and Cokes made it hard to process what was happening. That's when he worked to get her jeans off. That's when she tried to escape from underneath him, which made him counter by pinning her wrists to the mattress.

All she could say was, "Please don't, Alex." She repeated it a number of times, but he was too strong.

She had always wondered what sex would be like, but she had never imagined it would take so long or be so violent.

Afterward she thought they were alone until she heard the other boys, one saying, "Let's party." Knowing what might happen next, she decided to play dead, and that's when she heard Alex say, "She's wasted."

Her next clear recollection was puking into some bushes beside Alex's car.

Later, in the Dunkin' Donuts parking lot, Alex wouldn't stop talking. He made fun of some girl who had taken off her top and jumped into the pool; he said he didn't even know Henry's friends; he asked if she wanted another muffin. He didn't look at her as he rambled on. All she wanted was to jump out of the car and run home, but she was in no condition to do that.

At her house, he said, "Do you want me to walk you to the door?"

Do you want me to walk you to the door? she repeated in her mind. *Do you want me to walk you to the door?* Was he serious?

After that night, he did his best to avoid her in the halls. She waited one whole week for him to call and answer the question she'd been obsessed with, the one that jolted her from sleep each night: *Why?*

Alex wasn't going to tell Josh or his other friends about the party, but they always expected a report, so he gave them enough details to make them go away. He was aware something had gone wrong that night, and he needed to move on.

It was nine p.m. but still about 70 degrees outside. A nice night, quiet and dark along the bike path that circled a large pond. Since the beginning of spring he had been going for a run at this hour. He had even jogged with Maura once, then made out with her by the pond afterward.

Before leaving for the path, he was almost hit by an old black compact that moved so fast he couldn't get the license plate number. He shook his fist and swore at the driver, but then gathered himself, breaking into stride as he headed toward the path. Halfway through his run, as usual, he stopped at a water fountain and, bending over, drank deeply. When he looked up, he spotted Maura. She was sitting on a large slab that kids fished from during the day.

Faint light from nearby houses made it possible to see her face, which was expressionless. She wore jeans, running shoes, and a white hoodie with the school's insignia on it. She was facing him, her hands concealed in the pockets of her hoodie. He thought about ignoring her and sprinting away, but he was curious, so he approached.

"I take it this isn't a coincidence," he said.

"No, it isn't," she said.

"I was going to call."

"No, you weren't."

She was right about that.

"Look, Maura, we only have a few weeks of school left, so let's be civil and remember the good times." A second later, he was sorry he had said that. It was a line that had worked before, but he needed something special for Maura. He should've been patient. He should've sized her up, guessed at her intentions, then worked that angle.

"Look," he said, "I've tried to be nice, but if you don't stop stalking me, I'm going to get a restraining order. You know my father can make that happen."

And that's when she showed him the gun.

* * *

Maura knew about Alex's nightly runs and his routine stop by the water fountain, so she wasn't surprised when he materialized on the sidewalk in running shorts and a T-shirt. But she wasn't prepared for what happened next. As he was stretching with his back to her, she started the Mazda and, in a moment of rage, sped by, nearly grazing him.

Scared, she turned down the first side street she saw, shutting down the engine and trying to calm herself.

She was glad she hadn't hit him. She didn't want to make him a victim. She didn't want to ruin her plan. It was better to scare him. No one would believe that she had threatened to shoot him on the bike path, of all places. And if he told anyone, she had already chosen a place to bury the gun. She would just laugh and act like he was crazy.

After regaining her composure, she drove to an empty parking lot by the path and walked toward a large rock near the pond, not far from the fountain. That's where she waited, feeling the gravity of the gun weigh down the pocket of her hoodie.

She wasn't surprised when he approached or when he

spoke casually to her, as if he were still in control. *The Gunslinger,* she thought, a rush of anger seizing her again.

But there was also something pathetic about him. He was so clueless, and for a moment, she almost ditched her plan. But how could she forget that night, how long he had taken, how often she had protested? How could she forget the laughter and the smirks from his friends at school? And then he had to make a comment about the "good times," as if speaking to a little girl. That's when she had no choice but to wave the gun in his face.

"Whoa," he said. "Is this a joke?"

It must be a toy gun, he thought.

But upon reaching her, he realized the gun was indeed real. He thought about running, but then remembered that this was Maura holding the weapon, and he knew the kind of girl she was. She had confided her fears and insecurities to him. *She doesn't have it in her to shoot anyone,* he thought. She was trying to frighten him. Yeah, that's what this was about?

"You didn't have to bring a gun if you wanted an apology, Maura," he said, trying to sound as coolheaded as possible.

"I want you to kneel," she said.

He decided to go with his hunch. "I won't do that, Maura. I'm going to turn and walk away, and you're going to put that gun down."

"I wouldn't do that if I were you," she said.

But he turned, anyway, and started toward the bike path. That's when he heard it: a metallic *click*.

At first he had trouble catching his breath, but then realized the gun was indeed empty, that his hunch about Maura was right. She was angry but she wasn't crazy.

So he kept walking, imagining what a gunshot might actually sound like.

As he continued toward the path, two more empty clicks broke the silence.

He smiled.

Would it be like fireworks, he thought, a hammer hitting a board a few inches from his ear, the crash of a boulder dropped from an extreme height?

He moved farther away, supremely confident that, at least for now, he would never hear one of those sounds.

But then he did.

HEARTBREAK

Joyce Carol Oates

1.

In the top drawer of my stepdad's bureau the gun was kept.
It was kept unloaded.

They were laughing at the rear of the house. My sister Caitlin with her laughter like shattering glass and my cousin Hunt Lesinger who'd brought his .22 rifle over at Caitlin's request.

Giving her lessons in shooting a rifle. But not me, not even looking at *me*.

Showing off for Caitlin, is how it was. And Caitlin showing off for him.

In the mirror above the bureau—a flushed blurred face. I had learned to look quickly away from that face for so often I hated what I saw.

Mr. Lesinger's (forbidden) gun in my hand! Heavier than you'd expect.

(My stepdad didn't like it when I called him "Mr. Lesinger"—that did sound weird. He wanted Caitlin and me to call him "Dad." He put pressure on us to call him "Dad." But that was the name of our actual dad so how could there be *two Dads*? There could not.)

They were down by the ravine. I hated it, they'd gone off without me another time.

Behind Mr. Lesinger's house was an acre-sized lawn like a field that descended to a ravine, and beyond the ravine was Mineral Lake that was shallow and weedy at this end so you couldn't swim and even young kids wouldn't want to wade out in the muck on a hot day.

In the ravine was a wrecked car all overgrown with weeds and vines. Years ago someone had crashed his car through the guardrail up on Herrontown Road on a rainy night. The driver and his passenger had both died in the accident, in the ravine in what was called a "fireball" when the gas tank exploded.

This had happened long ago, before we'd moved into Mr. Lesinger's big shingle-board house on Herrontown Road. Before Mom had married Mr. Lesinger and brought us to our *new life*.

Mr. Lesinger hadn't told us about the ravine or the car. It wouldn't have crossed his mind probably. Adults don't think of the most obvious things like what's behind your own house, in a ravine. Part of Mr. Lesinger's property was marshy and you wouldn't want to walk there.

The ravine was about twenty feet deep, and part of it was filled with trash. You could hardly make out the wrecked car covered with vines and badly burned, that looked like the skeleton of a giant insect. Hunt Lesinger, who was Mr. Lesinger's nephew, knew about the wreck of course and the first time he came to visit us, after we'd moved into his uncle's house, he told us to come with him, he'd show us something we maybe didn't know about. It was a surprise to see the wreck back there, hidden from sight unless you knew what to look for.

First, we peered down at the wreck from the top of the ravine, which was dense with underbrush. Then, Hunt wanted to climb down. He'd brought his .22-caliber rifle that he left on the ground, for it was dangerous (he said) to climb anywhere with a rifle.

Caitlin hadn't wanted to climb down into the ravine—of course. But I was eager to follow Hunt.

Our stepcousin was the kind of boy you wanted to impress, by keeping up with him. Whatever he was doing. And if Hunt made jokes, you'd want to laugh.

It was awkward pushing through the underbrush, then slip-sliding down the rocky hill into the ravine. I'm a strong girl and my legs are hard with muscle but it was not easy going. A flurry of mosquitoes buzzed around my eager, damp face.

Caitlin cried, "Wait for me!"

Caitlin was wearing flip-flops on her skinny white feet, short shorts, and a tank top. Caitlin was so *girly*, you wanted to laugh. You wanted to give her a swift hard slap to make her stop acting so silly.

"You never saw this? My uncle never told you?"

Hunt recounted how he'd been in sixth grade when the car had plowed through the guardrail, and it was in the local paper and on TV. His uncle had said how he and his wife had just gone to bed at about eleven p.m. and they'd heard the car hit the guardrail, then the crash in the ravine, without knowing what they were hearing, and then the terrible loud explosion when the gas tank blew up—"Like the end of the world."

Of course, both the bodies had been removed. There was no trace of anything human in the wreck (that I could see) that had turned black in the fire. All the windows were broken but little slivers of scorched glass remained in the frames like teeth. If you tried to climb inside the wreck, you could cut yourself pretty bad.

I thought of climbing into the front, behind the melted-looking steering wheel and the black-burnt dashboard, to sit on what was left of the seat and pretend to be driving, but decided against it when Hunt shook his head *No*.

"Better not, Steff. You could hurt yourself."

Caitlin wouldn't come too near the wreck—her flip-flops were so flimsy on her feet, she couldn't risk climbing down into the ravine. Saying in her throaty little-girl voice (the way she never talked around the house but only if there was someone special to impress) she was afraid of seeing something "awful" (like bloodstains? parts of bodies?), how terrible it must have been, those poor people skidding in their car on the road, and crashing through the guardrail—"They must have been screaming all the way down."

Hunt said they didn't have much time to be afraid, the gas tank had exploded within seconds.

Hunt laughed, the way a guy will laugh when he knows he has said something disturbing. There are some thoughts that scare you so, you have to laugh.

Caitlin put her hands over her ears as if this kind of talk upset her delicate nerves. "Oh Hunt, *please*. I don't like to think about it."

It was like that with my sister. The least thing she could turn to her own advantage, to draw attention to herself, she would. But Hunt could see through her, I think. He'd just laughed as he and I were climbing out of the ravine, and didn't even answer her.

Later he said to me, "Maybe don't tell my uncle or your mom we were climbing in the ravine, okay? Just, they don't need to know."

It was thrilling to me, that Hunt would say this to me, in a quiet voice like we would share a secret.

His name was Hunter—everybody called him Hunt. It was a nice name that suited him. And he was an actual *hunter,* too.

He was my cousin—I guess you'd say *step*cousin. First

time we met, introduced by my mother, I knew Hunt and I would be in each other's lives forever.

"Steff, this is Hunt. You know—your new cousin . . ."

"Hi, Steff! Good to meet you."

Hunt was smiling at me, and it was a sincere smile. Hunt was not laughing at me. His eyes didn't slide away like guys' eyes do when they see, seeing you, that there's nothing to hold their interest but they need to appear polite.

Just then, Caitlin came downstairs. Even before Mom introduced them I saw how Hunt's eyes slid on my sister with her red-lipstick mouth and platinum-blonde hair streaked with just-visible strands of purple and green.

In that instant, when Hunt lifted his eyes to Caitlin, I could see how he was forgetting all about me.

I hated Mom calling me *Steff* instead of *Stephanie* which is a much more beautiful name.

Steff makes you think of *Stuff*.

I think it is a deliberate thing they do, my mother and my sister, and everybody else, to put me down. Not *Stephanie* but *Steff*.

But when Hunt said "Steff" it didn't sound so awful.

Hunt and his father, Davis Lesinger, had driven from

Keene, New York, in the Adirondacks, in his father's Jeep, to Morgantown, Pennsylvania, which is six miles south of Erie in the western part of the state. It was a twelve-hour trip they took once a year at least. The Lesingers were all hunters, and Hunt and his father had brought two hunting rifles with them.

Hunt was proud to show us his rifle, which was a Remington .22 caliber with a handsome polished stock—he brought it with him everywhere he could, he said.

Hunt's rifle was a registered hunting rifle. It was a legal gun in every way. When I saw Hunt lift it and squint through the scope I felt a chill along my spine but it was a pleasurable chill, of excitement.

Right away Caitlin said, "I want a shooting lesson! Ple-*ease*."

Hunt looked at Caitlin, and Hunt looked at me. It was like he was about to wink—at me.

Isn't your sister silly? How can you all stand her?

"Well, see—a rifle has a kick, Caitlin. It can hurt your shoulder if you don't handle it right. And the shot is loud."

It was startling to hear—how Hunt spoke the name *Caitlin*. So that it sounded special.

In this way, Hunt put my sister off. But knowing

Caitlin, how stubborn and persistent she was to get her way, I knew this would be just temporary.

Hunt's mother was no longer in their family, it seemed. Hunt did not explain where she had gone and we would not have wished to ask our stepfather Martin Lesinger who disliked personal questions especially from Caitlin and me.

"Maybe he's just like us, Steff! Except his mom left, not his dad."

Every summer Hunt and his father made the long drive from Keene to visit relatives in Morgantown. They stayed with his father's elderly parents for a week or ten days. It was strange for us (Mom, Caitlin, me) to think that they'd been coming to Morgantown all these years but we'd had no idea they existed.

Now that our mother had married Martin Lesinger, who was Hunt's father's younger brother, we were Hunt's relatives, too.

It was a surprise to Caitlin, and to me. I mean, a nice surprise.

We had a brother Kyle who didn't live with us. (Kyle lived with our father.) But no other close relatives in Morgantown, or anywhere. No cousins our age. Suddenly there was Hunt Lesinger in our house and my mother laughing at the looks in our faces. "Girls, this is your *step-cousin*. Hunter is *family*."

Whatever else was said at that time passed by me in a roar. Must've been blood beating in my ears.

Seeing Hunt for the first time, and seeing how Hunt smiled at me, it was like something turned in my heart. Like one of those tiny keys you can hardly grasp with your fingers but when you do, unlocking a lock, a little door comes open.

I had never seen any boy that age, or younger, or older, as polite and well mannered as Hunt Lesinger. Mom had told us he was eighteen years old—he'd graduated from high school three weeks before. In the fall he had a scholarship to study forestry at the state college at Syracuse. He was a tall, lanky, long-limbed boy with chestnut-colored hair and a habit of whistling under his breath. He laughed a lot, but not loud or rudely. His favorite things to do (he said) were hunting, hiking, canoeing, and camping in the Adirondacks. He hoped to work for the Adirondack National Park service after he graduated from forestry college. In the fall he planned to enlist in the New York State National Guard.

Mom kept saying how cool it was, she had a "nephew" now—a "*step*nephew." When she'd married Martin Lesinger eighteen months before she'd been hurt that almost no one from the Lesinger family had come to the wedding though most of them lived right here in Morgantown.

Mom's new husband was eleven years older than Mom. He had been Mom's boss at the Buick dealership where she'd worked until they were married, and you could see that he was still Mom's boss—the way he spoke to her, not exactly giving orders, never forgetting to say *Please*, but in a tone of voice that meant there was no negotiating.

Of course, Martin Lesinger had been married before. His wife had died of some wasting disease like Parkinson's—there were pictures of her in the house, which Mom intended to hide away as soon as she dared. But Mr. Lesinger's children were all grown up and none of them lived in Morgantown, or had troubled to come to the wedding. Caitlin and I felt funny thinking how we had *stepsisters* and a *stepbrother* old enough almost to be our parents whom we had never seen. That was weird.

Mom told us these *stepsiblings* were "not overjoyed" about her marrying Mr. Lesinger, whose wife had died just three or four years ago.

We asked Mom if these *stepsiblings* were worried about Mr. Lesinger leaving money to her and not to them? And Mom said she didn't think so, or anyway they shouldn't worry since she'd signed a *prenup*.

"What's a *prenup*?" I asked, and Caitlin turned to me with a sneer: "'Prenuptial,' Steff. Everybody knows what a 'prenuptial' is."

The way Caitlin said *Steff* made me want to slap her. Like my name wasn't a serious name and could be shortened to some ugly syllable while her name was such a special name, she would not allow anyone to shorten it to "Cate."

Mom explained to me what a *prenuptial* was. A kind of legal contract Mr. Lesinger had asked her to sign, to acknowledge that she would receive a "fixed sum" in the event of his death, and would be allowed to continue to live in Mr. Lesinger's house though she would not be the legal owner of the house, while the estate would be divided among the Lesinger heirs.

This did not sound right to me. Caitlin said she'd rather die than sign any contract like that—"If a man loved you, he wouldn't ask you to sign."

Mom's face reddened as if she'd been slapped. She told Caitlin she was speaking in ignorance. "There are different kinds of love. One day you'll find out."

But Caitlin just laughed and walked away, as if Mom was the most pitiful case she'd ever seen.

Did I hate my sister Caitlin? No.

Did I want to hurt my sister Caitlin? No!

Mostly this was a happy time for our mother, after a long unhappy time. It was a happy time for Caitlin and me, too—at least, it was meant to be.

We lived in a bigger house now, on three acres of land edging Mineral Lake. We had a *step*father now, not just a *father who'd abandoned us* (as Mom used to tell anyone who'd listen). Instead of a *dumped wife* Mom had become a *new wife*.

Mom was proud of her new name: *Mrs. Martin Lesinger*. In the kitchen I found a piece of paper with *Mrs. Deborah Lesinger* and *Mrs. Martin Lesinger* written on it a half-dozen times in red ink, which I ripped up and threw away. Embarrassing!

Caitlin and I still had our old name, which was our

father's name—*Doherty*. When he'd had a few beers Mr. Lesinger spoke of adopting us which made Caitlin laugh, and made me want to run away and hide.

Caitlin was sixteen. I was thirteen. *Too damn old to be adopted.*

Anyway, could a man adopt another man's kids? Was that legal? Even if Dad had left us and moved a thousand miles away (as Mom was always accusing) he was still our father, and *Doherty* was our name.

It was just after my eleventh birthday that Dad left. Later he said he'd waited until then on purpose, so as not to spoil my birthday on March 5. (But every March 5 after that would be poisoned by the memory. Funny Dad hadn't thought of *that*.)

Dad told us he'd left not because he'd stopped loving us—that is, Caitlin and me—but because *Your mother and I no longer make each other happy.*

That is a scary thing, I think. As soon as you fail to *make a person happy*, they can leave you.

We knew that Mom and Dad had been arguing a lot but we had not taken it too seriously. For a long time they'd been arguing about the least little thing you could imagine, like who had gotten gas for the car last or who'd left the thermostat too high. Or, when Dad spilled something in the refrigerator, he'd called for Mom to come clean it up. Without giving a thought to cleaning it himself.

Near as Caitlin and I could figure, our parents never argued about anything real at all.

Of course, we didn't know what they argued about when they were alone in their bedroom at the rear of the house. When they shut the door to that room with them inside.

In a family, one day is not so different from any other. Especially when you are very young—a "child." The important thing in life is routine. You can depend upon routine. There is comfort in routine. There is even comfort in the boredom of routine, for where there is boredom there cannot be fear.

Then one day, when Mom was at work, and Caitlin and Kyle and I were at school, something happened that had not ever happened before: Dad came back to the house in our absence, methodically packed his things into suitcases, backpacks, and boxes, and left.

Just left. Like that. And never came back.

It was hard to forgive Dad for telling Kyle beforehand.

So Kyle was not so stunned. But Caitlin and me, and of course Mom, were really stunned.

Some shocks, you never get over.

Each morning when you wake up there is a sliver of time before you remember what it was that has happened, that cut your life in two so you have thought *I will never be happy again.* So for that instant you can be happy. But then your memory sweeps over you like dirty water and of course you remember what it is, or was—what it was that had happened, that cut your life in two and can't be changed.

Dad moving out was like that. When we came home and he was gone it was like some kind of scene in a movie, where people are made to look like fools for being so taken by surprise. Being shocked, starting to cry—an audience will laugh at you for being so clueless.

Afterward I could not remember how we learned where Dad had gone. Maybe Kyle told us. Or, Kyle told Mom. I think it was that—Kyle took Mom out onto the porch to tell her. Must've been something like *Dad is gone and says he isn't coming back. He says not to try to get in contact with him.*

Kyle was such a jerk, we could not ever forgive him. To

keep from crying he kept making stupid jokes.

Of course we could see that Dad's things were gone. He'd swept his clothes out of the closets—his big jackets, in the front hall closet—so roughly, other things had fallen to the floor that he hadn't taken time to hang back up, or hadn't noticed. Not until the next morning did he call Mom, by which time Mom was in a very bad state.

It would turn out that in an argument Mom had told Dad, "If you're so damned unhappy all the time, just move out. We won't miss you!"

Mom had said such things in the past. Mom had sometimes screamed such things in the past. But Dad hadn't seemed to take it seriously, he'd just say something harsh and hurtful in reply, and it was soon forgotten, like water rushing along a riverbank. Except this time Dad had decided not to forget.

"Your mother told me to move out"—Dad would tell us, with a smirk—"and so I did. Hope she's happy now."

Saying such things meant that Dad wanted Caitlin and me to take his side against Mom. And maybe we did, sometimes. But we had to live with Mom and not with Dad, who didn't have room in his life for us (he said) but who'd agreed to take Kyle (there were special circumstances with Kyle).

Mom would say, in disgust *Your father has abandoned us*. She'd say *Your father is a rat abandoning a sinking ship*. But she'd try to laugh to show that this was a joke, sort of.

Hearing that the family would be "split," I seemed to see something like a great tree that has been split down its center with an ax.

For a long time Mom refused to speak of Dad at all. If she had to refer to Dad she would say *your father*. If she was speaking to someone else she would say *The girls' father*. (As if Kyle, who wasn't living with us then, did not exist.) Mom's lips twisted like there was a bad taste in her mouth, or she was trying hard not to cry.

In this way our lives that had seemed so familiar and so routine became strange and shaken up and complicated like a snarled ball of yarn. When Dad first left there were four of us left behind—Kyle, Caitlin, Mom, and me. Dad was supposed to see Kyle, Caitlin, and me on weekends except Dad's life was "difficult to schedule" and often he had to cancel; sometimes, he just didn't show up. Much of the time we had no idea where he was living, whether he was living alone or with someone. At one point he'd moved so far away, to Port Oriskany in New York State, it was a round trip of two hundred miles, so coming to see us, to pick us up to take us to a movie and supper, was a hassle and Dad tended to blame us for it. Mom was having issues with Kyle "acting out" (Mom's term) so she and Dad decided that Kyle should live with Dad, at least temporarily, so Kyle went to live with Dad in Port Oriskany and started school there but then Dad moved again, back to Pennsylvania, to Jamestown which was closer to Morgantown at least. By this time Kyle was out of school but living at home and trying to get work. And then Dad got "remarried."

This was a real shock to Mom. Such a shock, you could surmise that Mom had (secretly) been hoping that Dad would return to her.

Poor Mom! Caitlin and I were ashamed for her then.

It sometimes happened, that people who'd been divorced would reconcile, and "remarry." It was a TV kind of happy ending. Though it happened so rarely you could almost say that it never happened, yet you wanted it to happen, you wanted to believe it might happen to you and your family.

Did I believe, sort of? Maybe.

But seeing how pathetic Mom was, I wouldn't have ever told her.

I was twelve years old and a tall "husky" girl for my age—almost as tall as Caitlin. I hid away to cry—I was ashamed of being so weak. I hated it when Caitlin cried, which was mostly to get her way, not out of actual sorrow or grief but to make people feel sorry for her and do favors for her.

When Mom cried it was angry crying. Tears spilled down her cheeks that looked scalding. You had to run away!

It was around this time that Caitlin bleached her hair, and put purple and green streaks in it. Caitlin got her ears pierced, and a silver piercing in her nose, and started wearing the kind of sexy clothes Dad wouldn't have allowed her. (Dad was always saying he knew what guys are thinking when they see a girl dressed in a provocative way—"And it ain't nice. Take my word.") Caitlin became pushy and snotty and took out her bad temper on *me*.

Used to be, we'd been friends. Now, we were barely sisters.

Like Kyle I had "issues" at school so they sent me to the school psychologist who kept pretending to be sympathetic with me, encouraged me to cry if I needed to cry, pushed a box of Kleenex at me, and tried to get me to admit that I "hated" my parents for breaking up our home; I had to hate my mother for sending my father away, and I had to hate my father for leaving. But none of this was true. The only person I hated was the psychologist.

I did not hate my parents at all. I felt sorry for Mom, and all I wanted was for Dad to come back; we would all forgive him.

Then one day some older kids were pushing me in the cafeteria line, and I pushed back, and a kind of flame ran through me—*I hate you. Hate hate hate you.*

Seeing the look in my face and feeling how strong I was, so suddenly, they were frightened of me. They backed off fast.

From then onward, I did not cry. Not even when I was alone in my bed. After a while Dad became someone I saw at a distance, his face was small and blurred and no longer had the power to make me cry like a pathetic little baby.

Mom had a new better-paying job at the Buick dealership out on the highway. She began to take care with her hair and makeup and she dressed stylishly as she had not troubled to dress in years. She was often excited and distracted when she came home from work, late; many nights she *went out for drinks* with her friends.

Some of these friends were men, and sometimes these friends stayed overnight at our house.

Caitlin said it was "gross" but better than Mom depressed and drinking alone. "Then we'd have to take care of *her*."

Mom began to go away weekends—Philadelphia, Atlantic City, Miami, New York City. Once, Las Vegas. Her friends were divorced men with children, in complicated relationships. Over a weekend there might be strangers for supper, and/or strangers who were houseguests; kids our age, or younger or older, who used our bathrooms, slept on our living room sofa or in sleeping bags on the floor, asked if they could use our computer. Mom was always chiding *Don't be selfish, girls—this is my chance at happiness. There's plenty of room for guests here.*

At Thanksgiving there were eleven of us crammed around the dinner table. Don't even ask me who they all were. In the high-decibel noise even Caitlin was kind of silenced. It was like a tornado had rushed through the world uprooting houses and throwing people together who didn't belong together and did not even know one another but it seemed imperative that they sit together at the same table and *break bread together* as Mom called it.

Which was why I'd promised myself *Never me. Never get married and never any kids for me.*

Then, that phase ended. For Mom was seeing Martin Lesinger "seriously," and Mr. Lesinger was her boss at work.

Caitlin whispered to me, "Ohh gosh! He's so damn *old*," but I thought it was maybe a good thing that Mom's new man friend was older than Dad which might mean that he wouldn't get restless and leave her the way Dad did. He'd be *old*, and more settled in one place.

And this turned out to be so.

2.

"Hi, Steff."

Hunt saw me wince, and understood that that name was hurtful to my ears. So he began to call me "Stephanie" which no one but some of my teachers called me, and my heart melted.

When I was alone I said the name "Hunt" aloud. I

did not dare say "Hunt" when another person could hear, including my *stepcousin*.

While Mr. Lesinger and his brother, Davis, from Keene, New York, sat together in the living room smoking and drinking beer and talking in lowered voices, Caitlin and I spent time with Hunt outside on the redwood deck.

It was a warm summer day and Hunt and Caitlin were in shorts but I was wearing my worn old jeans, to hide my thick thighs.

Mom says that I am *not fat*, just *big-boned*. Mom doesn't have a clue.

Caitlin and Hunt did most of the talking. Half the time it seemed like they'd both forgotten I was there.

It was like Mom to fret over the simplest things. You could see that Mr. Lesinger and his brother had a lot to talk about, in private, for a while at least, and didn't want Mom hovering over them offering drinks and things to eat. And every few minutes Mom would come outside laughing and breathless to see how we were.

"What can I get you, Hunt? Another beer?"

"No ma'am. I'm fine."

"I'm thinking of making some cheese puffs. Y'know what cheese puffs are? Think you'd like some?"

In her whiny voice Caitlin intervened: "Mom, Hunt isn't hungry. He just had lunch. We're going target shooting in the ravine, he's going to give me lessons."

"No. I don't think so. That is not a good idea. Martin would not like it."

Mom spoke vaguely, not really listening to herself. All the while she chattered at us she was attuned to the men in the living room as if fearing they might be talking about her. Or worse, not talking about her at all.

In the bright sunshine Caitlin's platinum-blonde hair gleamed. Except for the purple and green streaks her hair was smooth and fine, and you had to concede that Caitlin was very good-looking, in a prissy spoiled way that I hated. For around Caitlin, everything had to be focused on *her*.

My hair was darker, a kind of muddy color. It was slightly coarse, not smooth, and my skin was slightly mottled, as if someone had rubbed it with a soiled eraser. It made me sick with resentment how Caitlin ate as much as I did, or almost, and was so sexy-skinny, while I was what Mom called *big-boned*.

Mom was always trying to make me feel better about myself. Using psychology, I guess. *Steff, your eyes are beautiful. Thick lashes like that, I wish I had . . .*

It was just bullshit. All I could do not to run away and hide.

Dad hadn't owned any guns but all the men in the Lesinger family owned guns. They were a hunting family, which was common in our rural county in western Pennsylvania, as it was common in upstate New York. Their favorite game was deer, which they talked about hunting, a lot.

I didn't like to think that my cousin Hunt, who was such a kind person, and so sensitive, could bring himself to actually shoot a deer! I could believe this of the other Lesingers, and of most men in fact, but not of Hunt.

Martin Lesinger owned not only a deer rifle but a double-barreled shotgun that he kept "under lock and key" in the basement of his house; and he owned a handgun, a revolver, which he told us was licensed for "homeowner's protection." This revolver he'd showed Mom, Caitlin, and me just once, to warn us never to touch it.

But then he added, "Unless there's an emergency situation. Someone breaking into the house when I'm not here. Someone who has to be stopped."

Mom laughed nervously at this remark. Mom said she hoped such an emergency situation would never come up since she had no idea how to shoot a gun and would be scared to death to touch his gun. And Mr. Lesinger said, with a smile, the way you forgive a silly person whom you love, "All you'd need to do is shoot at the ceiling, Debbie. Or at the floor. Any intruder would get the hell out of here, seeing you with a gun." Mr. Lesinger laughed as if that was a comical thought, and Caitlin and I laughed too.

This gun, which was a ".45-caliber automatic," as Mr. Lesinger described, he kept in a table beside his bed, unloaded.

Hearing this, Caitlin dared to ask what good would an *unloaded gun* be? If you needed a gun for an emergency, you'd need it loaded. Like, if Mom had to shoot at the ceiling.

It was like Caitlin to pipe up with some skeptical remark. I saw how Mr. Lesinger stared at her as if he'd have liked to slap her. I didn't understand why he was so annoyed by her for asking this question—which seemed like a sensible question that I'd have asked myself except I was too shy around Mom's frowning new husband—unless maybe there was something we didn't understand. *Because the gun is not unloaded, see? Of course, the gun is loaded.*

This was complicated. Mr. Lesinger wanted us to stay away from his gun or—we had permission to use his gun? The gun was unloaded, or—the gun was loaded?

Even Caitlin backed off asking more questions. Mom was smiling at all of us, obviously confused and waiting for the scene to be over—in her new marriage there were lots of scenes, like TV scenes, you found yourself in but mostly just waiting for them to get over. And Mr. Lesinger made me nervous when there was an edge to his voice.

When a man is irritated, it's like he might flail out with his fists. Not hard, and not to hurt, not even on purpose, but he just might do it, reflexively, and you might get hurt if you are standing too close.

And if a man hurts you, and you show that hurt, and your eyes lock with his, he will never forgive you. For always you will be the girl he *has hurt*, which means you are the girl he *can always hurt again*.

Mr. Lesinger put the handgun away in the drawer of the table by his side of the bed, shut the door firmly, and said, "There!"

We were not sure what *There!* meant. But the scene was over.

* * *

In Mr. Lesinger's house on the first floor and in the basement TV room there were mounted deer heads. These were "bucks" as Mr. Lesinger explained. It seemed like more, but there were just three.

The smallest "buck" looked very young, and his antlers were not nearly so large as the other bucks'. Caitlin murmured to me, *Oh gosh. I feel sorry for the deer.*

I felt sorry for the deer, too. It made me sick to think of anyone shooting such beautiful animals. Why didn't the damn Lesingers shoot themselves?—except for Hunt, I mean.

When we'd first moved into Mr. Lesinger's house we felt spooked by the mounted heads. Peering up at the deer's eyes you would swear were actual eyes, and not glass. And a deer's soul inside, peering right back out at you.

I am not so different from you. Why did you kill me?

I didn't kill you. It was a hunter.

But why?

I don't know why. I guess—hunters hunt. They like to kill.

3.

That afternoon, Hunt came to our house with his .22 rifle for target practice. Also, stolen away from a family barbecue at his grandparents' house, two six-packs of beer, a giant bag of tortilla chips, and some grilled (but still blood-leaking) hamburgers in soft doughy buns.

"Oh Hunt! What'd you *do*!" Caitlin was thrilled.

They laughed together like young kids. Hunt looked at Caitlin the way I'd dream a boy might look at me—not just smiling and friendly but seriously *looking*. Like there was something in Caitlin's face that seemed to trap him; he could not look away.

Caitlin was wearing short shorts and a pink tank top, and her midriff was showing, and part of her flat little belly. It was disgusting to see her so damned smug about herself.

I'd tried to wear a tank top last summer but Caitlin told me it was embarrassing, I was just too fat. Mom scolded her for using the word *fat* but to me she said, "Caitlin is rude, but she has a point. You don't have the figure yet for that kind of clothing, Steffi." Trying to placate me by saying *Steffi*, not *Steff*.

Trying too to be hopeful suggesting that one day, not

too far in the future, it might be suitable for me to wear the kind of tight, skimpy clothes my sister wears. If I was lucky.

We were alone at Mr. Lesinger's house—Hunt, Caitlin, *Steffi*. The adults (including Mom) were across town at Hunt's grandparents' house where there was a family barbecue in the backyard. Caitlin and I had been invited, sort of, but in such a way Mom had suggested we not come. Poor Mom had no choice but to accompany her husband and hope that someone in his family would take pity on her and talk to her about some other subject than how they missed Martin's deceased wife, Evvie.

Hunt had only lingered at the barbecue for a while before driving to our house in his dad's Jeep as (I guess) he'd planned with Caitlin. It wasn't clear if his dad knew he was coming over to our house or if anyone knew.

Later, the Lesingers would express total surprise and shock that Hunt hadn't been at the family barbecue. They'd seen the boy, they would claim.

No one had seen him slip away and back the Jeep out of the drive.

Caitlin put the hamburgers in the refrigerator for the time being. Hunt opened beers for all three of us but I couldn't swallow more than a small mouthful, the taste was so strong and so bitter. When I started choking, Caitlin and Hunt laughed at me.

"Steff's way too young for beer, Hunt. She's 'under-age.'"

"Yeh? What about you?"

"Not me. I'm just the right 'age.'"

They laughed together, excluding me. I was starting to hate both of them so hard it hurt.

Hating is hurtful. In the region of the chest.

Dressed like she was, and in flip-flops, Caitlin looked like some sort of silly sex doll. You could see the tops of her small white breasts and something of her skinny white back and her wrists were so skinny they looked like you could snap them like a twig. And laughing in that way that sounded like shattering glass, to rivet Hunt's attention. I'd never seen Caitlin *perform* so even on those nights Dad took us out to supper, and we were thinking (maybe) if we could win Dad over, he'd come back home.

We were out on the redwood deck just hanging out. I had the thought that Caitlin and Hunt wanted to be alone, but Hunt, at least, was too polite to say so. In his backpack he'd also brought a video—some episodes of

Game of Thrones, which Mr. Lesinger forbade us to see on his TV. Caitlin was saying we could watch it later, after target practice. While it was still light, she wanted Hunt to give her a lesson.

It was so, my sister was good-looking. Those wild streaks of color in her hair, and her shining eyes, you could see why a boy like Hunt would look at her like he did.

The thought came to me—*Maybe he will shoot her. Maybe the gun will go off wrong. That will shut her damn mouth.*

Oh but I didn't mean this! I was shocked to think it.

Just a crazy thought that came into my head like some kind of vapor and evaporated almost at once. It was hardly articulated in words. It was not a thought that belonged to *me*.

Hunt opened another beer for himself. Caitlin was gamely trying to finish hers. We were eating tortilla chips and Caitlin changed her mind about the hamburgers—"Maybe we're hungry now." She looked at me like I should know how to react to this remark.

I said that I would heat the hamburgers in the microwave. There was some ketchup in the refrigerator I could bring outside. I was eager to volunteer to be useful—I liked to be helpful when I could be. As if I wanted people to like me, even if I did not like them, as if I wanted them to think that I liked them. Or maybe—*maybe I did like them, and badly wanted them to like me.*

So I went into the kitchen and microwaved the hamburgers for one minute—found the ketchup in the refrigerator and some cans of Coke—some pickles, relish—leftover potato salad Mom had made the day before—and all this I brought outside on a tray, with paper plates and napkins, and salt and pepper in little crystal shakers that'd been filled (I seemed to know) by the woman who'd been Mrs. Lesinger before Mom. And when I pushed open the screen door—awkwardly, hoping I would not drop the tray (Hunt and Caitlin would really laugh at me then) and stepped onto the redwood deck—I was shocked to see that there was no one there.

I was just so surprised, I guess my mouth hung open.

"Hi? Hello . . . ?"

I had to suppose they'd gone down by the lake, or by the ravine (where else could they get to, so fast?) but there was no one in sight. It was weird, maybe it was comical; I set the tray down on the picnic table, walked from one end of the redwood deck to the other, looking for Caitlin and Hunt, calling, "Hi? Hey? Where are you?"—kind of pathetically saying, "Your hamburgers are ready. . . ."

It occurred to me that they'd hidden around the side of the house. In the garage? In the TV room in the basement?

All that I knew was, they hadn't come into the house through the kitchen. At least I knew that.

Steff! You're looking kind of lost.

This was so exactly what my mother would have said, I almost seemed to hear it. Mom's voice close in my ear.

But Mom wasn't there, no one was there. No one had spoken.

Where Caitlin and Hunt had got to—I just couldn't figure. If they'd gone back to the ravine, that was a kind of a long walk for them to get there so quickly, unless they'd run. (But why would they run? Why would they run away from *me*?)

Looking kind of lost. That was a sad thing for Mom to say, but it was true. Mom was always scolding me for being not "well groomed" like Caitlin (she'd say *other girls your age* but I knew she meant Caitlin) but I guess deep down she loved me, and felt sorry for me. But when people are nice to me that's when I cry, and feel really bad. And so I said, "I hate them both. I wish Caitlin would fucking *die*."

This was shocking to Mom and me both. This was the first time I had ever said such a thing even to myself.

Mom looked at me in amazement. *Watch that mouth of yours, girl.*

I turned away so that Mom could not see. My mouth was working but no sounds came out.

You know, we don't allow the f-word in this house. That's crude and vulgar and your sister knows better too and if your stepfather heard he would be disgusted. And if anybody hears, they will think you are a lowlife. You should be ashamed.

Some minutes, then I called, "Caitlin? Hunt?" I trotted all the way to the edge of the lake, where the soil was marshy and kind of smelly, and over to the ravine, where tall weeds and saplings were so thick you could barely see the wreck below. I could see that they weren't in these places but still I called, "Caitlin? Hunt?" like a fool. If this was TV people would be laughing at me. An invisible audience would be laughing at the fat girl *looking lost*.

I returned to the redwood deck, and around the side of the house to the driveway there was Hunt's dad's Jeep, which had not been moved.

(I'd had the sudden fear that they'd driven away in the Jeep, and left me. Maybe they'd decided to go to the Lesinger barbecue but had somehow forgotten *me*.)

But then, I went into the house. It had not occurred to me that they might have entered the house by the front door, and might be somewhere inside the house.

But they were nowhere in the first-floor rooms. No one here except the mounted deer looking at me pityingly. *Lost girl. Lost like us. Trophies on the wall. Pathetic.*

I was sweating now, and breathing quickly. I was feeling so ashamed!

I stopped calling "Hunt? Caitlin?"—reasoning that if they didn't hear me call them, they couldn't be blamed for not answering me; but if I continued to call them, and it was clear that they heard me, it would also be clear that they'd played a trick and hidden from me, and that would be mortifying.

I went back out onto the redwood deck, and they still were not there. A fly was crawling over one of the hamburger buns but I was too distracted to chase it away.

Caitlin's beer bottle had been set down on the picnic

table. I think the bottle had to be Caitlin's—it was just half full.

There were at least two empties on the table. These had to be Hunt's. (But had he had a third, in his hand? Had he walked away with this bottle?) The bottle from which I'd taken just a sip or two was where I'd left it on the flat railing top.

I snatched this up and took another swallow. So bitter! But I managed to keep it down, out of spite.

They'd gone somewhere, and Hunt had taken his beer bottle with him. Maybe. (I saw now, Hunt's rifle was lying on the deck, where he'd placed it. And his backpack. These had not been moved.)

I wondered if I should wait for them to come back? Obviously they had not gone far.

Obviously it was some sort of joke. On me.

Not a mean joke, just a joke.

"Yo, Steff! Hiya."

Suddenly there came Hunt's laughing voice—and Caitlin's high-pitched laughter.

They'd been downstairs in the TV room, after all. There was an entrance to the basement around the side of the house that I guess I'd forgotten. I stood there on the deck blinking and confused, but after a minute I was relieved to hear myself laughing.

Laughing so hard it hurt my belly. For I'd managed to finish the bottle of beer, and I was feeling—well, weird.

What do they call it? *Buzzed*.

Hunt and Caitlin were telling me (like they expected me to believe this!) that they'd decided to experiment with the TV, or the DVD player, just to see if it was operating. "For later, when we watch the video." Hunt was carrying a beer bottle, in fact. His smile was lopsided and boyish and his words were slurred.

"Like, we might want to stream a movie. If the DVD doesn't work out."

Why was Hunt telling me so much? Like it seemed important to him, that I would believe him.

I opened another beer for myself with the bottle opener. The little cap went scuttling across the floor of the redwood deck and we laughed, seeing this.

We sat at the picnic table and ate the food I'd set out. Caitlin wasn't very hungry for the lukewarm hamburger—"Damn, Steff, this is hard as a rock! What'd you do to it?"—but she drank the Coke thirstily. Hunt devoured two hamburgers soaked with ketchup and more than half the potato salad. "Thanks, Steff! This is great."

Steff. He hadn't even noticed what he had said, that he'd picked up from my sister.

Caitlin said that meat was *gross.* Eating animal muscle and tissue was *gross.* She'd been thinking, maybe she would become a vegan.

"Meat is protein," Hunt said. "Vegans get skinny and sick."

"Caitlin is skinny already," I pointed out.

It was an inane remark but everyone laughed including Caitlin.

Then, Caitlin said, "Steff, is there ice cream? In the freezer?"

"No. I don't think so."

"Maybe—go look?"

There wasn't any ice cream in the freezer. Mr. Lesinger had a weakness for ice cream so he forbade Mom to buy it. Sometimes we were allowed to have frozen yogurt, but there wasn't any frozen yogurt in the freezer, either. Caitlin might not have known this or was pretending not to know.

It was a signal for me, to go into the kitchen and check. To bring a container of ice cream out onto the deck, and three spoons.

So I went inside, but had to use the bathroom. And when I came out of the bathroom I checked the freezer, which was crammed with packages of meat and leftovers but no ice cream.

I found some gingersnaps in the cupboard. On a high shelf, where Mr. Lesinger asked Mom to put them, so he couldn't reach them easily, or he'd finish the entire box. These, I brought outside.

This time, as soon as I stepped out onto the deck, I saw the two of them walking away—not hurrying, and not glancing back—toward the ravine.

"Hey? Hunt? Caitlin . . ."

Hunt was carrying his rifle slung over his shoulder. Caitlin had talked him into giving her shooting lessons. If Mom knew, she'd have been upset. Mr. Lesinger wouldn't have liked it, either. The mean thought came to me— *Caitlin will get in trouble now. They both will.*

On the deck I stood watching them, thinking my thoughts. The beer helped me think more clearly. *I am not going to chase after you again.*

Instead, I cleared the picnic table. Like I didn't give a damn about them, or had even noticed them. Damn buzzing flies! Ketchup-soaked napkins, Caitlin's shredded hamburger and bun. Smeared mayonnaise from the potato salad on all the plates. And the empty beer bottles, and tortilla chips crushed underfoot.

I hate you so. Hate hate hate you so, wish you were both dead.

I thought that I would behave responsibly, as Mom might do in such a situation. When Dad had said awful things to her, and made her cry, she'd retreat to the kitchen to clear away dishes, to clean up. Sometimes she'd scour the stained linoleum, squatting on her haunches on the floor.

We avoided Mom at such times. Caitlin, Kyle, Steffi.

Poor Mom! She's pathetic.

Just stay out of her way.

Inside the kitchen I could watch them from a window. They were at the ravine now, just standing there. I tried to imagine what they were saying to each other, but I could not. Without me, they would talk of things I could not imagine. This was so painful to me, I was drinking a second, maybe a third bottle of beer. The buzzing at the back of my head was louder now, and exuded a yellow light. Almost, I could see that light if I shut my eyes.

I heard a shot—had to be Hunt with his rifle.

Desperately I thought, *I am not chasing after you. Not ever again.*

Upstairs in the big bedroom where Mom and Mr. Lesinger slept, on Mr. Lesinger's side of the bed was the table, and inside the drawer was the gun.

Never touch. Except emergency.

I saw myself opening the drawer, and I saw my hand lift the gun out—it was *heavy.*

Really, I was just watching. The buzzing at the back of my head had spread to the front part by my eyes and I was watching what I did through this buzz, that was like fluorescent lighting.

The gun in my hand, *.45-caliber automatic.* There was something scary about it but comforting as well. Like, something so heavy in your hand, and your hand was given a certain distinction.

If this was TV, or a movie close-up. The girl's hand, and the girl herself, at which you wouldn't wish to glance for more than a second, given a certain distinction.

I did not think—*Is the gun loaded?* For some reason that thought did not occur to me at all, as I had not (somehow) thought that my sister and my cousin might've hidden from me in the basement TV room, when the door was right there around the corner.

Some things, you just don't think. Though later you would realize these were the first things that you should have thought.

It seemed to take a long time to hike to the end of the field that prissy Mr. Lesinger liked to call a lawn. The sun was hotter than before and my eyes were beginning to get blurry.

Hunt and Caitlin weren't at the ravine now but over by the lake standing in the marsh where cattails grew to the height of a man's shoulders. There was trash here, too, which had spilled over from the ravine in a heavy rainstorm. Hunt was sighting along the barrel of his rifle, aiming at something in the lake—a glittering patch of water. He fired, and Caitlin gave a little squeal of fright. But it was insincere fright, you could see.

Caitlin wasn't eager now to take the rifle, I guess. She'd liked flirting with Hunt but when it came to actually taking the rifle from him, she wasn't so sure.

I called out to them, "Hey! Hi! Look what I have!"

Hunt turned, and when he saw the gun in my hand he didn't seem so welcoming as I had imagined. And

Caitlin was looking shocked.

I'd thought my cousin who loved guns would be impressed by this gun. I'd thought for sure he would be impressed with *me*.

"Steff, for God's sake! What is that—a gun?"

Caitlin was shocked but also disgusted. She didn't seem to notice my flushed face, which felt hot and swollen. The buzzing in my ears was like a roar.

"Is that—*his gun*? You took out of his bedroom? Oh my God."

Hunt was trying to smile at me, but I could see that Hunt was also disapproving.

"Is that my uncle's gun, Steffi? Maybe you should put it down."

I told Hunt that I wanted a gun lesson, too. I wanted to learn, too.

Caitlin said, "That is not a plaything. That is Mr. Lesinger's gun. You put that right back where you found it. We won't tell anyone but you'd better do that—now."

I knew my sister would say this. Or something like this. It was like Caitlin to spoil anything I wanted to do, when I was poised to be happy for once.

I did not mean to do anything but scare Caitlin. She

was so mean to me, and seemed to be ashamed of me. The mistake was, I know that it was my mistake but it was also Caitlin's mistake, that she was so nasty to me. She was sneering, and stuck-up, and full of herself, and she didn't give a damn about me. When we were with Dad, she got all the attention from him. Like all the light in the room, or all the oxygen in the room, and didn't care about me, and how lonely I was.

So disgusted, looking at me as if she shouldn't have been scared of me. Respectful of me.

For I had Mr. Lesinger's gun, which I had to hold in both hands because it was heavy. And I was pretending that it was loaded.

I was pretending that it would really shoot if I pulled the trigger. "Get down! Get down on the ground, you are arrested!" I was mimicking cops on TV programs, like *Cops*, that's what the cops always shout at the pathetic whiskery drunk men they're trying to arrest. *Get down! Get down on the ground!* The men are slow to obey sometimes out of defiance but sometimes because they are dazed and drunk and disbelieving. Sometimes they are even half-naked—bare-chested, and barefoot. Ridges of fat at their waists spilling over their belts. You see them on TV and feel revulsion for them, which is a disgusted kind of pity. *What do his children think! Does he have a daughter? How can she show her face at school? She is more shameful than I would ever be.*

Caitlin was saying mean, sharp things to me. Caitlin was threatening me she'd tell Mom and Mr. Lesinger about me. Caitlin was sneering like she didn't even know me, I was so far beneath her. Caitlin came forward to slap at me, or to take the gun from me—that is what I remember.

And the gun going off—that is what I remember.

How I was ducking away in the marshy grass, and the mud was sucking at my feet. And the gun must have shifted in my hand. The direction of the barrel shifted. In that moment I seemed to have no control over it, the gun was too heavy, it is not like the idea of a gun that is exciting but the actual weight and feel of a gun, that is something different. For maybe Caitlin did not rush at me and try to slap me, but I would remember the look of disgust in her face. And Hunt looking kind of surprised and scared and he's saying, *Stephanie, hey—don't aim that at us.*

Hunt was reaching toward me, and Hunt had pushed

Caitlin back, behind him. As if to shield her. Shield her from *what*! I was furious seeing this, because there seemed to be a misunderstanding. And it seemed that I would be blamed. I shut my eyes. I did not pull the trigger but—the gun went off.

There was a loud *crack*! Mr. Lesinger's gun went off by itself and jerked from my hands and fell into the mud.

I knew then, something terrible had happened. It wasn't my fault, it wasn't Hunt's fault. If there was any fault it was Caitlin's, but Caitlin would not be the one who was punished.

Saw Hunt on his knees in the marsh grass, and that look of shock and hurt and fear in his face. And blood like a burst dark flower on his T-shirt, high on his chest. And Caitlin screaming. And my screaming, too—I think it was me screaming.

4.

"Stephanie?" The voice is firm but kindly.

In this place there is an air of acceptance, unsurprise.

There is not what you'd call trust, exactly. I see in their faces, in their eyes, that they are not comfortable with me, or with other court-mandated juveniles who are like me, though they may feel kindly toward us, and they are accepting of us as *outpatients* receiving court-mandated therapy. We are *work* to them, and they are *working* to make us well.

I have not told any of the staff at the clinic that I am sick with heartbreak. I have told them that I am very sorry for what I did, though with a part of my mind (it is possible that the more experienced among the staff can "read" this part of my mind, but I pretend that I don't know this) I don't truly think that what happened was my fault, or my fault entirely. *My sister! My sister is to blame.*

Hunt did not die. But Hunt took a long time to recover, after emergency cardiovascular surgery to save his life.

Hunt would not be enlisting in the New York State National Guard, or in any of the armed services. Hunt would probably not be strong enough to hike, hunt, camp in the mountains as he'd loved to do.

I would not ever see Hunt again. I knew this.

Soon after the "gun accident" (as it was called), I was sent away to live with my father and his new wife in Jamestown, Pennsylvania.

Partly this was because Mr. Lesinger did not want me in his house any longer, ever again. But also, Caitlin had come to truly hate me. (She had not hated me before, I realize now.) And Mom seemed fearful of me though she insisted that she was not and that she loved me *just as much as ever*.

It was thought best that I go away to live somewhere else where (mostly) no one knew me. A new home, a new school district. In the Morgantown family court it was decided that as a first-time juvenile offender I would receive *psychotherapy* and *counseling* as an outpatient. I would not be *incarcerated* in any facility.

Dad has full-time custody of me now though I think he is not so happy with this arrangement, and I know that his wife is not at all happy. And even Kyle is fearful of me, at times.

For I have become one of those persons of whom others will say—*There is something not right about her. Be careful of her.*

Even if they don't know who I am, and what I did, or caused to happen, in a "gun accident" when I was thirteen years old. Even if they don't know that I am sick with heartbreak they will say of me—*That one, Stephanie. Just be careful around her.*

It is really true, something is wrong with my heart. I

can't breathe deeply the way I once did, my chest hurts. I can't sleep more than an hour or so at a time—something just wakes me up, like a slap. I hear a girl's sharp, scolding voice—I hear a girl screaming. And I sit up in bed, gasping for breath. In the dark I am anxious of what the day will bring. Sometimes I see a dark ravine with something glittering deep inside it. There is a lake, and there is no opposite shore that I can see, but it is known to me that if I can swim to that shore, I will be all right again and my cousin Hunt will love me again.

In this place, I am so lonely. But I am lonely in all places for I carry my loneliness around with me like a heavy backpack.

No one calls me *Steff, Steffi* any longer.

ABOUT THE AUTHORS

MARC ARONSON: Marc is a passionate lover of nonfiction, a devotion he expressed as an editor (of the tenth Robert F. Sibert Medal winner and YALSA Nonfiction finalist), author (first Sibert Medal winner and YALSA Nonfiction finalist), and professor at the library school of Rutgers University. He enjoys working with other authors and has now collaborated on seven books. Marc frequently speaks to professionals and students throughout the country. See www.marcaronson.com for more information.

EDWARD AVERETT: Edward is the author of *The Rhyming Season* and *Cameron and the Girls* (Clarion Books). His short stories have appeared in the collections *Rush Hour: Bad Boys* and *Every Man for Himself.* Mr. Averett hides away in North Idaho and Ecuador with his wife, Mary. Visit him at his website www.edwardaverett.com.

FRANCESCA LIA BLOCK: Francesca is the author of more than twenty-five books of fiction, nonfiction, short stories, and poetry. She has received the Spectrum Award, the Phoenix Award, the ALA Rainbow Award, and the 2005 Margaret A. Edwards Lifetime Achievement Award as well as other citations from the American Library Association and from The *New York Times Book Review*, *School Library Journal*, and *Publishers Weekly*. Her work has been translated into Italian, French, German, Japanese, Danish, Norwegian, Swedish, Finnish, and Portuguese. Francesca has also published stories, poems, essays, and interviews in the *Los Angeles Times*, the *Los Angeles Review of Books*, *Spin*, *Nylon*, *Black Clock*, and *Rattle*, among others. In addition to writing, she teaches fiction workshops at UCLA Extension, Antioch University, and privately in Los Angeles, where she was born and currently lives. Visit her online at www.francescaliablock.com.

CHRIS CRUTCHER: Chris is the author of ten critically acclaimed novels, an autobiography, and two collections of short stories. Drawing on his experience as a family therapist and child protection specialist, Chris writes honestly about real issues facing real teenagers today. He has won three lifetime achievement awards: the Margaret A. Edwards Award, the ALAN Award, and the NCTE National Intellectual Freedom Award. Chris lives in Spokane, Washington. Visit him online at www.chriscrutcher.com.

ALEX FLINN: Alex registered as a Democrat because her high school government teacher told the class it was a waste to register as an Independent. She never looked back. She is the wife of a shooter, and the author of eleven novels, including *Breathing Underwater*, and the number-one *New York Times* bestseller *Beastly*. Her newest book, *Mirrored*, is a retelling of the Snow White story. She lives in Miami. Visit her online at www.alexflinn.com.

GREGORY GALLOWAY: Gregory is the author of *The 39 Deaths of Adam Strand* and the Alex Award–winning *As Simple as Snow*. He earned his MFA at the Iowa Writers' Workshop, and his work has appeared in *The Iowa Review*, *Rush Hour: Reckless*, and McSweeney's Internet Tendency. He was taught to shoot as a boy by his uncle, Dr. R. K. Willms, who took him deer hunting for the first time. At the time of this publication, he has never shot a deer or any of his friends.

JENNY HUBBARD: Jenny, who was a high school English teacher for seventeen years, now spends her days writing in her hometown of Salisbury, North Carolina, where she lives with her math teacher–husband and their rescue schnoodle. Her first novel, *Paper Covers Rock*, was a finalist for the prestigious William C. Morris YA Debut Award, and her second novel, *And We Stay*, earned starred reviews from *Kirkus Reviews*, ALA *Booklist*, and *School Library Journal*. For more tidbits on Jenny visit www.jennyhubbard.com.

PETER JOHNSON: Peter's fiction and poetry have received creative writing fellowships from the National Endowment for the Arts and the Rhode Island Council on the Arts, along with the Paterson Prize, and a "Best Children's Book" citation from *Kirkus Reviews*. His most recent novels are a YA thriller, *Out of Eden*, and a middle grade novel, *The Life and Times of Benny Alvarez*. He can be found at www.peterjohnsonya.com.

RON KOERTGE: Ron writes fiction for young adults and poetry for everybody. His latest novel-in-verse is the very well-reviewed *Coaltown Jesus*. His latest book of poems is

The Ogre's Wife. A devoted handicapper, he can often be found around the paddock at Santa Anita racetrack. He lives in South Pasadena, California, with his wife, Bianca Richards. Visit him online at www.ronkoertge.com.

CHRIS LYNCH: Chris has been publishing YA and middle grade books for over twenty years. Titles include Printz Honor–winning *Freewill*, National Book Award finalist *Inexcusable*, and a five-volume series on young men in the Vietnam War. He will have three books coming out in 2015: *Killing Time in Crystal City*; *Hit Count*; and the sequel to *Inexcusable*, which is titled *Irreversible*. He teaches in the low-residency creative writing program at Lesley University and divides his time between the east coast of Massachusetts and the west coast of Scotland.

WALTER DEAN MYERS: Walter, who passed away in 2014, was the *New York Times* bestselling author of more than a hundred books for readers of all ages. Much honored, Walter's novel *Monster* was the recipient of the first Michael L. Printz Award. He was also a recipient of the Margaret A. Edwards Award for Lifetime Achievement and was the first recipient of the prestigious Coretta Scott

King–Virginia Hamilton Award for Lifetime Achievement. He also authored two Newbery Honor Books and six Coretta Scott King Award–winning titles, and was a three-time National Book Award finalist. From 2012 to 2013 he served as America's National Ambassador for Young People's Literature. Learn more online at www.walterdeanmyers.net.

JOYCE CAROL OATES: Joyce is a recipient of the National Medal of Humanities, the National Book Critics Circle Ivan Sandrof Lifetime Achievement Award, the National Book Award, and the PEN/Malamud Award for Excellence in Short Fiction, and has been nominated for the Pulitzer Prize. She has written some of the most enduring fiction of our time, including the national bestsellers *We Were the Mulvaneys*; *Blonde*, which was nominated for the National Book Award and the Pulitzer Prize; and the *New York Times* bestseller *The Falls*, which won the Prix Femina Étranger 2005. She is the Roger S. Berlind Distinguished Professor of the Humanities at Princeton University and has been a member of the American Academy of Arts and Letters since 1978. In 2003, she received the Common Wealth Award for Distinguished Service in

Literature, and in 2006, she received the Chicago Tribune Literary Prize for lifetime achievement. Visit her on Twitter @JoyceCarolOates.

ERIC SHANOWER: Eric is the award-winning cartoonist of the graphic novel series Age of Bronze, retelling the story of the Trojan War. He is the writer of the comic book series Little Nemo: Return to Slumberland with art by Gabriel Rodriguez, based on the classic comic strip Little Nemo in Slumberland by Winsor McCay. With cartoonist Skottie Young, he adapted six of L. Frank Baum's Oz books to a series of *New York Times* bestselling graphic novels. Eric's past comic work includes his own Oz graphic novel series available as Little Adventures in Oz and art for *An Accidental Death* by Ed Brubaker, *The Elsewhere Prince* by Moebius and R. J. M. Lofficier, and *Harlan Ellison's Dream Corridor.* He has illustrated for television, magazines, and children's books, two of which he wrote himself. He lives in San Diego, California. Visit him online at www.ericshanower.com.

WILL WEAVER: Will grew up in northern Minnesota. An outdoorsman and "thoughtful hunter," he is the author of many novels for young adults, including *Memory Boy* and *Saturday Night Dirt*. One of his short stories was adapted into the feature film *Sweet Land*. Visit him online at www.willweaverbooks.com.

ELIZABETH WEIN: Elizabeth writes fiction for young adults. She is the author of *Code Name Verity* and *Rose under Fire,* as well as the Lion Hunters cycle set in Arthurian Britain and sixth-century Ethiopia. Her newest novel, *Black Dove, White Raven*, combines her love of flying with her fascination for Ethiopia. Elizabeth was born in New York and grew up in England, Jamaica, and Pennsylvania, and now resides in Scotland, where she has lived for over fifteen years. She is married and has two teenage children. Visit her online at www.elizabethwein.com.

TIM WYNNE-JONES: Tim has written thirty-three books for people of all ages and sizes. He has won Canada's Governor General's Award twice and been nominated five times. He has also won the Boston Globe–Horn Book Award twice, most recently for his YA thriller *Blink & Caution*. He has twice won the Arthur Ellis Award of the Crime Writers of Canada and once won the Edgar Award presented by the Mystery Writers of America. His books have been translated into a dozen languages. He was nominated for the Hans Christian Andersen Award in 2012. That same year, Tim was made an Officer of the Order of Canada. Visit him online at www.timwynne-jones.com.